COMPENDIUM

THE HORROR CHALLENGE COLLECTION

ISBN: 978-0-9839069-6-4

Cover Concept, Artwork and Design: JH Glaze
Text Editing: Susan Grimm
First Printing July 2013
Published by MostCool Media Inc.
"Make it interesting. Make it MostCool."

Proudly printed in the United States of America.

First Edition July 2013

10 9 8 7 6 5 4 3 2 1

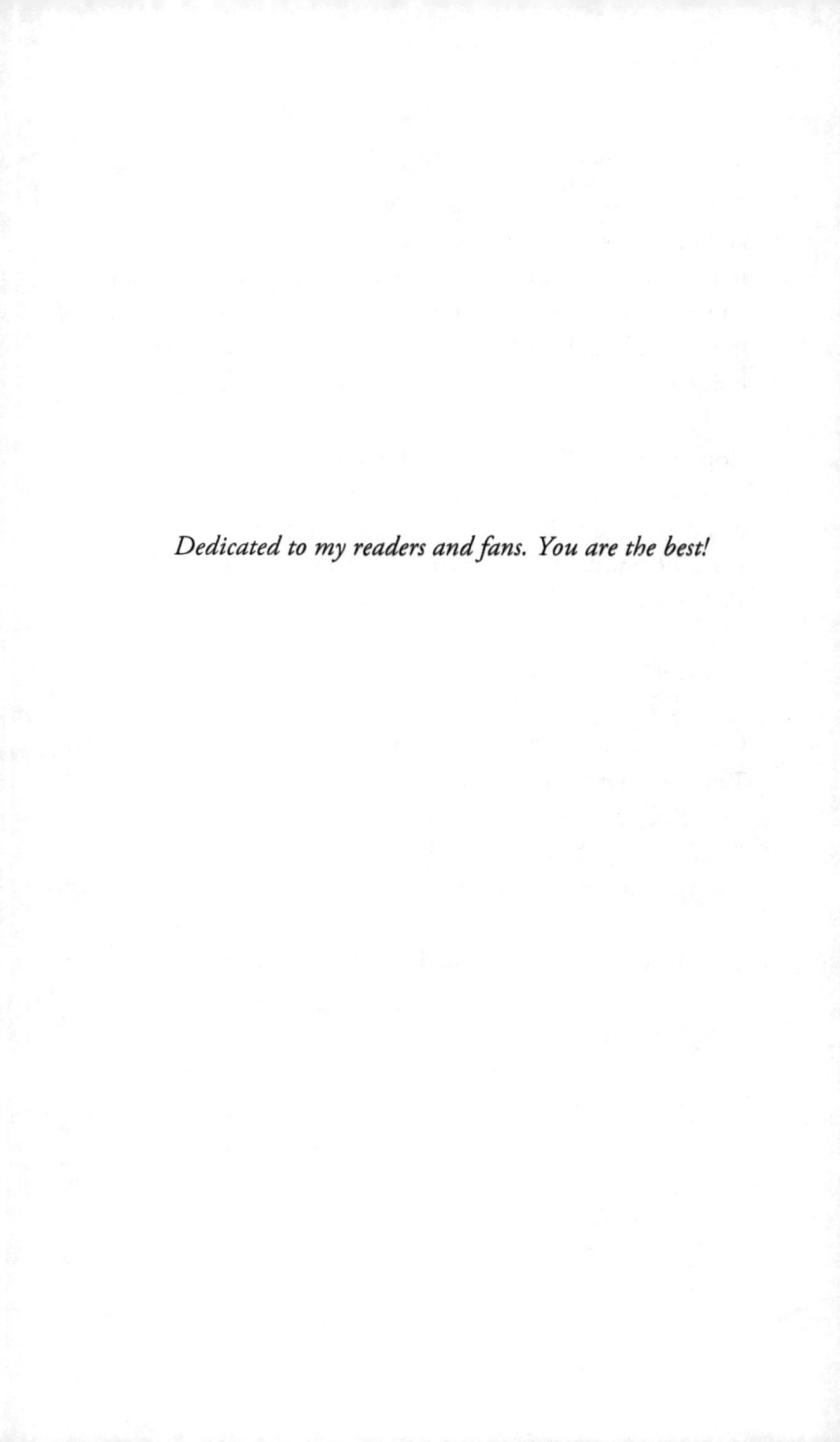

Dedicated to my readers and fans. You are the best!

This book is a collection of three eBook volumes of The Horror Challenge. The series was developed as a way for readers like you to directly suggest topics of one or two words for stories, making you a part of the creative process.

The words or topics submitted are used in an original story. For some stories, I combine several suggestions for a more interesting outcome. When the stories have been written, they are published along with the name of the person who suggested the topic and the word or topic that was suggested.

I hope you will enjoy these stories as much as I enjoyed writing them. If you would like to be a part of future projects, visit my Facebook page, The Horror Challenge, and submit your suggestion. All I need is a word or two and I will twist it into a story from there.

"I enjoy writing fiction. It gives me the opportunity to make things up that I have never seen, to create enemies I've never known, and destroy them in grand battles with weapons that don't exist. Life is good."

J.H. Glaze

Horror Challenge Topic Suggested by:
Angie Edwards – A Piano

SPOOKY

When Sarah's mother passed away, she was tasked with settling her mother's estate. After the service, and with her mother finally laid to rest, the time had come to hold a sale to liquidate all of her mother's possessions. The money from that sale would hardly make a dent in the mountain of debt that her mother had left behind.

The sale was to be held the next morning, and she planned on spending a few last hours in the house before heading to her hotel for the night. With the help of an estate sale professional, she had spent the day sorting and discussing the prices of every item in the old house, including her mom's upright piano.

That piano held many memories for Sarah. From the time she was six years old until midway through high school, she had taken piano lessons. She had practiced many hours at those worn yellowed keys while mom did the dishes. Without fail, she would call to Sarah from the kitchen, "Play Spooky, honey."

In fact Sarah had played that song so many times that after all these years, it was the only song she actually remembered. So now here she was, getting ready to sell this old thing.

"Mom, if you're there, I'm going to play Spooky for you one more time before I sell the piano. You know I don't have room for something this big in my apartment." She was looking around the room as if she expected her mom to make an appearance, but nothing happened.

As she slid the bench out to sit down, it came rushing back to her. Even the smells of her mother's cooking filled her nostrils and she recognized her favorite – macaroni and cheese.

Sarah slowly opened the lid to expose the keys, sat there for a moment with her eyes closed and began to play. She was surprised that her fingers seemed to remember every note as they drifted over the keys. In her memories, she could hear her mother singing along from the kitchen. She came to the third verse that contained these lines…

"If you decide someday to stop this little game that you are playing

I'm gonna tell you all the things my hearts been a-dying to be sayin

Just like a ghost you plan on haunting my dreams …"

And as those words were sung in her mind, she stopped playing and sat staring at the keys.

Suddenly the piano began to move beneath her fingers. A vibration at first, it began to shake violently to the point that it was lifting nearly six inches from the floor. Sarah jumped up, knocking the bench over as she stood, and backed away from it.

She heard the piano wires clanging as it was being torn apart. Then in a last violent heave, it lifted several feet off the floor and crashed to the ground. As it hit, it fell apart and the side panels fell off.

Sarah stood staring at the mess, wondering if what she had seen had really happened. If it had, was it over? After a minute, she noticed something green sticking out from under one of the panels. She cautiously moved toward it and grabbed the wooden panel moving it away from the rest of the shattered wood.

She stood in shock at what she had uncovered, stacks and stacks of banded hundred dollar bills. It was more money than she had ever seen in one place at any time in her life, and much more than it would take to pay off all of her mother's debts.

As she stood there crying, she heard a distant voice she recognized as her mother's as she sang the last line of the song:

"Love is kinda crazy with a spooky little girl like you."

Horror Challenge Topics Suggested by:
Wanda Hart – A Vanity Mirror
Julie Miller Janney – An Aquarium

MIRROR, MIRROR

Seven-year old Angie was fascinated with her new spaceship shaped fish aquarium. Mom had purchased it for her at the Pet Emporium last week along with Wally, her black and orange speckled goldfish. So excited at having her first pet, it had been difficult to find just the right place for it in her room. Finally after much deliberation, she had settled on the vanity where she sat to brush her hair when getting ready for school each morning.

She'd hated that vanity when she had first gotten it. She was only five, and forced to give up her giant toy box in order to make room for it in her tiny bedroom. Since then she had come to enjoy it and all of the drawers where she could keep her most favorite treasures.

The vanity had only one mirror, unlike the larger one owned by her friend. Wanda's had three mirrors and was given to her after Wanda begged her mom to get her one too. Angie didn't care. Wanda didn't have a spaceship fish tank and she wasn't about to tell her where mom got it. If she did, Wanda would probably ask her mom for one of those too. No, the fish tank would be her private secret.

On Tuesday, Angie came home from school to find a long mirror had been installed on the wall in her bedroom. Mom said that since she was a big girl now, she would need a wall mirror to see how she looked before she left the house for school, saying, "You'll understand when you are older, how important it is to look nice for school." But for now, it was just taking up the space where she could have put up another Lady LayLa poster.

Angie sat down at her vanity to talk to Wally about it. "What should I do Wally?" She put her face close to the side of the tank, "Mom says I have to leave the mirror up, but it's so big, and I wanted to put something else there." As she talked to the fish, she tried to see the mirror on the other wall reflected in the mirror of her vanity, but she couldn't see the other mirror from that angle.

Being a determined little girl, she decided to turn the vanity rather than to simply turn and sit sideways. "Hang on Wally", she said grabbing the corner of the vanity and pulling it hard until she could see the mirror behind her.

"Wow, look at that!' she exclaimed as she witnessed for the first time the 'tunnel effect' created by the opposing mirrors. "It looks like it goes on forever!" She moved back and forth, watching the tunnel move back and forth into infinity. "Hey, Wally! I know what we can do!" She turned the small fish tank so the front of the spaceship pointed at the mirror behind her. "You can fly your spaceship through the tunnel!" and she got down so her head was at the same level as the tank so she could see what it would look like.

As Angie moved her head slightly back and forth, she imagined Wally flying through space in his rocket. He appeared to be navigating as he swam back and forth. As she watched, there was a flash of light in the mirror on the other side of the room and she thought she saw something. It was big and dark and it scared her enough to make her stand straight up and yell, "MOM!"

Angie ran from the room continuing to call out for her mom. She ran down the stairs and into the kitchen, but mom was not there. She looked through the glass of the back door and saw her out in the garden cutting flowers. She opened the door and ran out to tell her what she had seen.

Meanwhile upstairs in her room, the small fish tank had begun to vibrate. Small waves formed on the surface of the water as the tank lifted off of the top of the vanity. At first it just hovered there with Wally swimming back and forth frantically. Then it shot forward in a blur toward the mirror on the wall and disappeared through the tunnel.

"Mom, there's something scary in my room!" Angie said breathlessly as her mother cut another flower stem. "It was in the mirror on the wall and it looked really big."

"Honey, you might be upset about the mirror, but you don't have to make up stories. You will be glad it's there in a couple of years."

"But, Mom, I'm not making it up! There was something up there! Come see." She grabbed her mother's hand pulling her toward the house.

Back upstairs, something large was coming quickly toward the small bedroom through the tunnel from the vanity mirror.

"Angie, please. Give me a minute to finish up and then I'll come and check…"

A loud crash came from the house as the window from Angie's bedroom was blown out. Broken glass and a massive flood of water poured from it and rained down on the shrubs below.

"What the…!?" Mom was running for the house now. As she grabbed the handle of the door and pressed the button to open it, the pressure of the water behind the door blew her back into the yard. She struggled to stand as Angie was frozen in place, pointing up toward her room. Her mother followed with her eyes to see the large black tentacles unrolling through the window.

Light years away in another universe, a young Grong male sat in his living pouch staring at the tiny object on the floor where only moments before his pet Flark had been swimming happily in its container. As he bent down to examine it, he saw a small orange and black speck moving around inside it and let out a wailing sound as he ran from the pouch to tell his mother.

As the Grong ran out, Wally continued swimming back and forth, oblivious to anything beyond his tank.

Horror Challenge Topic Suggested by:
Gillian Schafer – A Toaster

FORGET ABOUT IT

Madge and Henry had been married for more than sixty years. Theirs was a model relationship and they were totally dedicated to each other. In their later years failing health affected them both tremendously, but they held their marriage vows as a solemn oath to each other. They had promised, in sickness and in health, and they cherished every moment together.

It was this bond that kept Madge going these days. After Henry's accident, she took to caring for him even though it had rendered him unable to speak or do anything for himself.

On this particular morning, she had prepared Henry's breakfast as always – eggs, bacon, and a biscuit with butter. He sat at the table as he did every morning, but for some reason he wasn't eating today.

She tried not to worry too much about it and went on with her chores, cleaning up the mess she had made. She put the butter in the cupboard, and cleared the table as Henry sat staring straight ahead. It was as if he couldn't see her or the care she exercised not to break anything as she worked. Her eyesight just wasn't as good as it used to be.

She cleared most of the table and though Henry hadn't touched his food, she took his plate and put it in the sink. "I guess you aren't hungry today, Mister... uh." It bothered her when she couldn't remember his name. To cover her embarrassment, she went back to her work.

She turned on the faucet and rinsed the two paper plates carefully. She didn't want them to fall apart like they did the last time. She pressed the handle on the toaster down and tried to place the first plate into the slot. It was too wide to fit. She had an idea and folded it in half so it fit nicely, then did the same with the second plate.

"I am almost finished here, dear. Then maybe we can go for a drive." She giggled at the thought of driving, she loved it so. Now that she had finished the dishes, she could look for her keys.

She left the kitchen through the door that led to the garage. She supposed she had left her keys in the car, but to her surprise someone had taken her car and left a pickup truck in its place. Now she was angry. She turned around and went back into the kitchen to ask Henry about it when the doorbell rang.

She decided to deal with the truck later and went to answer the door. There was a young woman standing there with a bag of groceries. She was smiling as the door was opening, but slowly her expression turned to a frown as she spoke. "Madge? Where is Henry?" she asked.

"Who? There is no one here by that name." Madge was confused. "How can I help you?" Right about then, a wisp of smoke floated from behind her, and straight into the face of the strange woman at the door.

"Is something burning?" She asked, gently forcing her way into the house. Frantically looking around, she saw the cloud drifting from the kitchen and ran to investigate.

Flames and smoke were pouring out of the toaster. Quickly she reached back and pulled the plug. She grabbed a towel, wrapped it around the toaster and set it in the sink.

As she lifted the towel, she saw the raw and rotting eggs and bacon coating the sides and bottom. She turned to question Madge and saw Henry sitting there staring at her.

The last scheduled visit had been a week ago to the day. Madge whimpered and muttered a little as she watched her examine Henry. It was hard to know exactly when he had died, but without his loving supervision, Madge had been lucky to survive the week.

Horror Challenge Topic Suggested by:
Eclectic Heathen – A Toothbrush

THE DENTAL PLAN

Carrie was eating her dinner later than usual this evening. Scott had called earlier to let her know he would be late once again, so she had taken her time deciding what to make. The growling from her stomach finally convinced her to eat something.

Today was Valentine's Day and she had a special surprise for her husband whenever he would finally arrive. She was determined that no matter how late he was, she would spring it on him. After all, this was more than just a day of celebration of love. It was the day he had proposed to her those eight years ago.

When she finished eating she went upstairs and showered, washed her hair and plugged in her curling iron. While she waited for the iron to heat up, she applied her makeup meticulously. She wanted to look as attractive as possible for him tonight. Everything about this evening had to be perfect.

She curled her hair and slipped into the special lingerie she had bought earlier in the week. If Scott didn't react positively to this, he must be really worn out from his day, she thought as she admired herself in the mirror.

Around eleven, she heard him pull his car into the garage. He came in through the kitchen, stopping for a drink, then headed up the stairs quietly so as to not wake her. He let out an audible gasp as he entered the bedroom. There was his alluring wife stretched across the bed like a girl from a centerfold in a men's magazine.

"Wow!" was all he said as he took in this vision of beauty. "Can you wait a few minutes while I get cleaned up? You look totally amazing." He was all smiles as he looked into her eyes.

"Sure, honey. Why don't I run a nice hot bath while you brush your teeth, then I'll wash you all over before we play." Carrie tried to keep her excitement in check as she walked into the bathroom.

As she bent to turn on the water in the large garden tub, she could feel him behind her standing at the sink. He turned on the faucet and took his toothbrush out of the container where he kept it soaking in mouthwash. He began to brush.

Scott was always obsessed with his gorgeous smile and he took great care to maintain it. He always said that brushing for a minute was good, but five minutes left his teeth their whitest. No need for chemicals.

Carrie sat on the edge of the tub watching as he put the toothpaste on the brush and began his ritual. She took note of the clock on the sink as it ticked through about four minutes before speaking. "I got a call a couple days ago, honey. It was kind of strange."

He looked at her in the mirror and mumbled, "uh huh," as he continued to brush. "It was your personal assistant and she told me quite a story. She said that you two were in love."

Scott stood frozen at the sink wide-eyed, the toothbrush still in his mouth. "She went on to say that you never really loved me anyway. I guess you told her that I'm rather demanding, which is why you were ready to leave me for her."

He didn't move he just continued to stare in the mirror while she finished. "That was bad enough honey but what really clinched the deal for me was the part about the diamonds you bought her for Christmas last year. You know the Christmas when you got me that nice bathrobe?"

He continued to stand there frozen, staring intently at the mirror. "Don't you have anything to say for yourself?" She reached down and turned the water off as it neared the top of the tub. Carrie laughed, "Oh that's right! You can't talk right now because all of your muscles have kind of seized up."

She walked over to him and grabbed him around the waist and eased him to the floor. She leaned him against the sink so he could see her while she spoke.

"You know when I have a lot of time at night alone, I can surf the web and learn a lot about a lot of things. It seems that this plant I got yesterday has a special poison that causes loss of muscle control, like totally. It dissolves easily in water and it's untraceable."

She sighed as she saw a pool of urine on the floor forming beneath him. "Don't worry baby I'll clean that up while you get your bath." With that, she put her arms around him and dragged him toward the tub. He had already removed his shirt and slacks so it was nothing to get him undressed completely.

As Scott lay on the floor totally naked staring at the ceiling, she stood over him where he could see her. "Okay, it's bath time! Oh wait. I forgot." She bent down and kissed him on the cheek and whispered, "Happy Valentine's Day, honey."

She put her arms around his chest and pulled him up and over the edge of the tub, carefully lowering him in headfirst. She lifted his legs over the side and took a minute to arrange him as if he had been bathing and accidentally slipped under the water.

His wide eyes revealed his terror, while the last bubbles of precious air escaped his nostrils. She took a towel out of the cupboard and laid it out as if he had prepared to dry himself, then used a dirty towel to mop up his mess on the floor. At the sink, the last thing she did was dump his container of mouthwash, rinse it with water, and replace it with some fresh mouthwash and his cleaned toothbrush.

As Carrie walked down the stairs, she yelled back up toward the bathroom, "I hope that bitch was worth it!" Downstairs, she went to the kitchen to open a bottle of wine. By the time it was gone, her alibi would be complete.

Horror Challenge Topic Suggested by:
Melissa M. Ringsted – A Lamp

ENLIGHTENMENT

Alan attended the auction for three hours and was determined to buy something from the antiques collection before the day was over. After all that time, he hated the thought of walking away empty handed. Finally, late in the afternoon, something came up that he could probably afford. It was an antique lamp.

The lamp was definitely old, although he wasn't so sure it was an antique. The other bidders must have felt the same because when the bid hit fifty bucks, he was the last man standing. As he stepped up to the table to pay for his purchase, he felt good about having won the bid. When they handed him the lamp, the woman behind him in line smiled and remarked, "Nice lamp."

As he drove home, he glanced at the lamp on the seat beside him and thought about the woman's comment. She was right. It was indeed a nice lamp. Somehow he felt as though he had seen one like this before. It seemed so familiar and that made him smile.

When he got home, he hung up his coat and began to look around for the right place for his new treasure. Ultimately, he settled on a small table next to his sofa. Seeing it there now, he wasn't sure that it fit with his minimalistic decorating scheme. He decided to give it time to settle into its new home. He unwound the cord from around the base

and dropped it to the floor while he went to get a light bulb
from the closet.

He returned with one of those twisty fluorescent bulbs in
his hand. Reaching down inside the shade, Alan screwed in
the bulb. He felt a small sense of excitement as he pulled the
cord to the wall and plugged it in. It was time to see if it
worked. He reached up under the shade and flipped the
switch.

It lit up nicely as he looked in at the bulb, but something
had changed. He thought he had just screwed in a
fluorescent bulb, but instead there was a regular
incandescent. He did a double take and stepped back and
realized that all of his furniture had disappeared. The room
was now filled with furniture that looked as though it had
been taken from the 1960s.

Alan began to feel kind of sick, so he sat down on the
brown sofa that had replaced his cool white leather. He
rubbed his eyes and looked around again. He couldn't
believe what he was seeing. This old furniture was arranged
exactly as he had arranged his, except there was a boxy
wooden television with a rounded screen on the floor
beneath where his flat screen had hung from the wall.

He thought he might be dreaming and there was one way to
prove it. He stood and walked over to the old television and
switched it on. It flickered to life, and soon he was looking at
an episode of The Twilight Zone. It was one of his favorites,
the one about a guy who finds himself alone with a library
full of books. He is really excited about having all those
books to read until he accidentally breaks his glasses. A real
classic and it was only half over.

He decided if this was a dream he might as well let it play
out, so he sat back down on the sofa to watch the rest of the

show. By that time, a commercial had come on. It was a man dressed in a suit really enjoying his smoke while the announcer talked about its smooth flavor.

Alan was so intrigued that he didn't notice the movement behind him. It appeared he had interrupted a burglary, and the burglar was creeping up behind him. Looking around for something to use as a weapon, the intruder grabbed the lamp off the table and hit Alan on the side of his head.

There was barely time for Alan to make a sound before the man began to hit him repeatedly. Ultimately, he lay dying on the sofa with the side of his skull bashed in. As his life slipped away, he could hear the final moments of his favorite show.

Alan opened his eyes and sat up on the sofa. He could feel the cool leather beneath him. He turned to look for the lamp, but it was gone. Maybe the whole thing had been a dream after all. He had a bad headache and needed to take something for it. As he stood and rounded the sofa, he saw the lamp lying on the floor. It was broken into several pieces and still plugged in.

Feeling freaked out, he got a paper bag and a broom with a dustpan. He picked up the large pieces of the lamp and swept up the rest of the mess. Emptying the dustpan into the bag, he carried it out to the trashcan in the garage.

Intrigued and a bit confused, he went back into the house and straight to his computer. He sat down and opened the search engine. He typed in his address and "1960's murder." A link to a local newspaper site came up on the screen.

He learned that a man about his age had been killed here in his house by a burglar in 1964. The thief had bludgeoned the victim to death with a lamp. He couldn't believe it. He had just experienced it in complete detail. As he read on, he became so immersed in the article he didn't notice the movement behind him.

Horror Challenge Topic Suggested by:
Lynn Worton – A Vase

A FINE COLLECTION

Jason sat at the bar sipping his martini as the vibration of the music pressed against him, thump, thump. The club was crowded tonight just the way he liked it and, as always, the odds were on his side.

He was a young man of striking good looks with his jet-black hair, green eyes, and a body that made him look like a model from one of those calendars for hungry women. So it was only a matter of time before he would meet someone, exchange some small talk, and follow her to her place for a few hours of wild lovemaking.

When the gorgeous woman standing before him had walked up to him from across the room, he wasn't surprised at all. His confidence had been unwavering since about the age of sixteen.

"I've been watching you from across the room," she began her introduction. "I must admit you look much tastier up close." She licked her lips with practiced coyness. "You have amazing green eyes, you know? The kind a girl could fall into and lose all track of time."

Did she really just use that cheesy line on him? "Oh yeah? Well, you look pretty good yourself." He took her in from head to foot, letting his eyes linger over her breasts for just the right amount of time before glancing back up at her smile.

She stood about five foot four, and she was just about the hottest girl at the club tonight. He figured if this turned out to be the one he went home with, it would be time well spent. Her blue eyes and long brown hair framed her timeless features in a way that compelled him to match her lusty gaze.

"Look, I really don't like clubs all that much." She moved closer so she wouldn't have to yell over the music. Leaning in, she spoke more quietly into his ear. "You wouldn't like to come to my place for a while, would you? We could get to know each other in a deeper, more intimate way." She leaned back to see the expression on his face, then back in to set her hook. "You wouldn't have to stay any longer than you want, but I would sure love to add you to my collection."

"Collection?" Jason was intrigued. "What is it you collect exactly?"

"Incredibly beautiful men, of course!" she said as she leaned in even closer and gently bit at his earlobe.

"Okay if we go now?" He was definitely ready.

"Uh huh, now," she said, taking his hand and pulling him toward the door. He let her pull him out the door and into the parking lot.

Outside, she insisted that he leave his car at the bar. She would drive him back as soon as he wanted or call him a cab if he preferred. There could be drinks involved in this arrangement, so he agreed.

Soon they arrived at her place, and he was amazed at the size of her penthouse apartment. He was quite impressed with her taste in decorating, with its fine silk furnishings and early Egyptian statues. It was like something out of a movie.

"Have a seat while I pour the wine," she offered as he marveled at the claw footed marble tables and the large vase sitting on the end table next to the sofa. Was it inlaid with real gold and rubies?

When she came back into the room and handed him a glass of wine, he couldn't help but ask, "Do you work for a museum or something?"

She shook her head and laughed, "Oh no, I inherited most of these things from my father. He was a famous archeological scientist in his day." She sat down next to him on the sofa, sipping her wine. "Wait until you see the bathroom! Drink your wine and I'll show you."

As he drank his wine, he could have sworn he heard her singing something quietly in a foreign language. Rather than ask her about it, he just finished the glass and set it on the table.

"Very good, Jason. Now wait a minute while I go straighten up the bed before we get started."

Something didn't seem right and after a moment he figured it out. Things had happened so quickly at the club, he hadn't asked her name or given his. So how did she know his name?

"You might be surprised what I know about you, Jason," her voice called out from the other room. "I know that you treat women like objects to add to your collection. You trade them and discard them at will." She was walking from the other room now as she continued. "And that my dear makes you perfect for my collection."

Jason was rather freaked out now and wanted to get up and leave, but his legs were tingling so badly that he didn't feel he could stand. His arms were weak, and he felt dizzy. He opened his mouth to speak and his jaw fell slack against his chest. He tried to close it, but nothing happened.

"I am sure you are wondering what is happening to you. I could explain it all to you, but we don't have that much time, so I'll make this brief." She sat next to him and took his rubbery limp hand in hers. "The short story is this: I slipped something into your wine, of course, and with a bit of magic and a few chosen words, I have set in motion a spell that will cause your bones to dissolve."

As she spoke, his spine seemed to melt and he slushed into a heap on the cushion of the sofa. She was careful to push him back to keep him from spilling onto the floor, then stood and looked at him. "I really do love those green eyes. Would you mind if I kept one of them to admire? Of course, you wouldn't." She laughed as she bent over him and plucked one of his eyes "You won't be needing this anymore anyway." It made a sucking sound as she pulled it out of place, then it snapped as the strands of muscles attached to it stretched apart and broke like a rubber band.

She set the eye on the table as she lifted the ornate vase and held the open end down against the blob that only moments ago had been Jason. Slowly, he was sucked into the vase like a Jell-o shot at a college party.

As she sat the vase back on the table, she smiled. "I think you'll get along just fine with the rest of the guys. You all have a lot in common." She picked up the slimy eyeball from the table and strolled into her bedroom to get some rest.

Horror Challenge Topic Suggested by:
Lisa Cagle – Recliner Chair

Bob Saves the World

Bob loved his recliner chair. It had been his throne for twenty years, so you can imagine how he felt when Carol drew a line in the sand and said with conviction, "That chair has to go!"

Sure, Bob had argued his case to the best of his ability. He had told her with tears welling up in his eyes, "But honey, it's been my wheels at NASCAR, my 747 as I traveled across the continents of the world, and even my Starship Enterprise while exploring the final frontier!"

Carol had laughed at him and walked away uttering the words that drove a stake through his heart. "The new chair is being delivered tomorrow, and I'm having them haul that smelly thing away."

So this was it, his last night as the king of the living room. He went to the refrigerator and grabbed a beer, then back to his chair. As he eased down into the well-worn cushions, he leaned back slowly bringing up the foot support. Then, using the remote control, he switched on the TV just in time for Star Trek reruns. How perfect to say goodbye to his old friend watching the same show he watched when it was sleek and new.

About ten minutes into the show, the Enterprise was under attack by Klingons. Kirk asked Scotty for more power, to which Scotty replied he was giving her "everything she's got…" Suddenly the sound from the television was muffled as a semi-transparent dome closed around the chair with Bob sitting in it. Immediately and at top speed, it shot straight up through the ceiling, the second floor of the house, the attic, the roof and right out into space!

Bob gripped his remote control in terror and the force of gravity pushed him so tightly into his chair that he couldn't even force a scream out of his lungs. In seconds, he was hundreds of miles above the earth and passing through the doors of a giant space ship. The chair came to rest at the feet of two very gray aliens with large black eyes.

Bob was afraid to move. He just sat there shaking and staring at the strange looking creatures until one of them "spoke" inside his brain. "We have studied your planet and have decided that it needs to be destroyed. However, we will allow you, as the spokesman for your race, one opportunity to redeem yourself and your world." The creature stopped, looked at the other alien, and smiled.

Then the second one was now speaking into his brain, nodding its head as it instructed him. "While studying your world, we have seen great battles resolved by the answer to a single question. I believe it is called Trivia and the victors seem to wield volumes of knowledge. Therefore, we will ask you one question. If you answer it correctly, your world will be spared." At that moment a three dimensional Earth appeared in front of the dome. "If you fail, you will be the only living witness of the destruction of your world."

Bob was stunned. How the hell could he possibly answer a question asked by creatures from some other galaxy? He felt panicked and feared that anything he might say would be wrong and his world could be obliterated before the question was even asked.

"Are you ready, human?" The voice boomed inside of his head. Sadly he nodded. It would all be over in seconds when he failed to answer the question correctly.

"Go on. Let's get it over with." He lay back in the chair and inhaled deeply trying to relax so he could think clearly.

The first alien asked the question, "What is the primary component of the warp drive method of propulsion? You have one minute." Bob could hear them both laughing, and it was a painful distraction.

"Could I have some quiet please?" he asked as he tried to remember every piece of junk science and fiction he had ever seen, read and heard. On the front of the dome appeared some type of timer that seemed to be ticking down the seconds. Bob could feel his heart pounding in his chest. His brain was frantically searching through the stores of his memory like Carol and her friends when they're shopping at a clearance rack. 'Oh my God, Poor Carol' he thought.

Suddenly, he remembered an episode of Star Trek where the engines had been damaged. A repair had been necessary, but what was the part that had required the repair?

The timer wound down its final seconds and the alien cheerily exclaimed, "Your time is up, human. Do you have an answer?" The gray creatures stood with their arms crossed over their chests. One of them was holding a large red button in its hand, its finger hovering at the ready to push it and destroy his world.

It was now or never, so he gave it his best guess. "The primary component of the warp drive method of propulsion is... the gravimetric field displacement manifold." He closed his eyes tightly. He didn't want to watch as the earth was destroyed. He would never see Carol again. He didn't see the shocked looks on the alien's otherwise expressionless faces.

They turned to each other, and then one began waving its arm toward the dome.

Bob felt himself falling fast and he thought he might die as he flew out of his chair and smashed against the top of the dome. Fire engulfed him and he was sweating as he saw the earth coming up fast. Just before he would slam into the ground, he saw his neighborhood, then his house. WHAM! The dome landed on the floor exactly where it had first appeared and Bob fell back into his seat.

The dome dissolved and disappeared just before Carol walked into the room. "I hope you are enjoying that nasty thing. I'm not kidding, it's gone in the..." She stopped, her mouth hanging open as she noticed the hole in the ceiling of the living room.

When she looked back at Bob, he was still sitting in his chair grinning as he answered, "Okay sweets, I think it might be time for a trade-in. This one does have a hell of a lot of miles on it!"

Horror Challenge Topic Suggested by:
Donna Lide Strickland – A Newspaper

READ ALL ABOUT IT

The newspaper was in the shrubs again. Paul had told the paperboy over and over to stop throwing the paper into the bushes. He wanted it up on the porch or he was cancelling his subscription. Honestly, he didn't want to cancel. He really liked reading the paper at breakfast, but it was getting rather old having to go into the shrubs every single day and coming away with his arms scratched up.

This was the day he was finally going to take a stand. He went back into the house and found the phone number for the paperboy under a magnet on the refrigerator. Then he picked up the phone and dialed.

"Hello?"

"Uh, is this Charlie's mother?" he was trying to calm himself.

"Yes, may I ask who is calling?" The woman sounded very nice, but he wouldn't let this deter him.

"Well, I'm one of his customers, Mr. Bishop. I want to talk to him about throwing my newspaper in the bushes yet again."

"Oh yes, Mr. Bishop. He's out in the driveway right now. I can relay a message if you like."

Paul took a deep breath, and then totally lost his composure. "Look, if that boy doesn't come over here right now and get that paper out of my bushes, I'm going to call the newspaper and ask them to fire him. Better yet, I'll demand it!"

"Well, Mr. Bishop. I'm sorry about that. Would you like me to tell him to do it right now?"

"Yes, I would!" he replied. "Otherwise his ass is grass, and I'm gonna be the lawnmower!" He realized that may have been a little too much, but he was pissed.

"I'll tell him, Mr. Bishop." She hung the phone up without saying another word. She didn't even give him a chance to apologize for sounding so harsh. Oh well, sometimes it is just as well. A long explanation could have been poorly received anyway.

As he waited for the boy, he made himself some coffee and sat down to drink a cup – without his paper. Fifteen minutes had gone by before he heard something moving out front. He got up from the table and walked toward his front door. He was going to give that kid a piece of his mind.

Paul could hear banging and crashing like someone was tearing up his porch. He set his coffee mug down on the end table and ran to open the door. As he stepped out onto the porch, he saw the paperboy fly up in the air from the bushes where he had been fetching the paper.

There was a screaming howl coming from some kind of large beast there. It was big and black and covered with long fur, and it was knocking the shit out of Charlie. It wasn't a dog. He'd never seen a dog that big. It was more like a bear or a lion or something he had never seen before. As it turned it's head to go after the boy again, he saw its giant mouth and rows of jagged teeth.

He had to do something. Looking around, he spotted a shovel leaning up against the side of the house. He grabbed it and ran down the steps. The boy was screaming, but his cries were fading. Paul moved fast, swinging the shovel and hitting the thing in the back.

With every swing of the shovel, he pulled it back again as the blood flew from the beast. His face and arms were soaked in the sticky red mess. He was sure he was hurting it, and soon he could free Charlie from the bushes and get him some help.

Suddenly from behind him there were screams from a woman who was walking down the street. The man who had been walking alongside her ran to get a better look at what was happening. There was a whimper coming from the bushes as the bloodied man was about to bring the shovel up over his head to land another blow. He sprang into action and tackled Paul in mid-swing sending them both tumbling. Paul dropped the shovel as he fell.

The man was an off duty police officer and he yelled for his wife to get him some backup as he held Paul to the ground. Paul was trying to argue that the beast in the shrubs had been ripping the boy apart, but all the cop saw was the lifeless, hacked up body of the local paperboy slumped over a shrub.

No matter what Paul said, there was no way to convince the man that there had been a vicious creature there. He knew he had been trying to save the boy. "I'm not crazy!" he yelled, struggling to get the man off his back. He may not have realized he had cancelled the paper months ago, but he knew the monster was real.

Horror Challenge Topic Suggested by:
Melissa M. Ringsted – Bad Customer Service

THE CABLE BILL

When Lainie opened the statement from the cable company, she screamed so loud she almost brought the house down. It was three times the amount of her previous bill. This month's bill showed an order of twenty movies, none of which she had actually ordered or watched. In fact, she rarely watched television at all since her hobbies took so much of her free time.

There was no way she was going to stand for this outrageous discrepancy, so she walked straight to the phone on the counter and prepared to dial customer service. She scanned the bill for the number, then hit the ON button and dialed. Two rings later, she was connected to a recording. "For English press one," and she did. "To report an outage press one. To order additional equipment, press two. To add premium channels, press three." Lainie was getting hot as she waited, and she fanned herself with the folded bill.

"To request new service, press four. If you are moving and need to request moving your service, press five. If you would like to check your current bill using our automated system, press six. If you need to talk to technical support, press seven." She was really about to throw the phone when, "If you need to speak with billing. Press eight." She pressed eight.

"Thank you for calling Beamed In Cable. All of our representatives are currently busy assisting another customer.

Please stay on the line and someone will be with you shortly." Then the music started. After about five minutes, a man finally answered. "Thank you for calling Beamed in Cable, how may I help you?"

"I need to talk to someone about my bill. Uh, I was charged for movies that I didn't order." There was silence on the other end. "Hello?" she said.

"Yes, I'm here. I'm pulling up your account right now. Please hold." Immediately the music was playing again. Lainie was pacing back and forth by the time the rep got back on the line. "I'm sorry, Mrs. Conway, but our systems are down right now. Tell me what your problem is and I'll make a note of it. As soon as our systems are back up, I will check into the problem. Go ahead."

She started, "Well, as I was saying, there were charges for twenty movies on my bill that I didn't order. I need for you to credit my account for them."

"There were twenty movies on your bill you didn't order?"

"Yes."

"That's a lot of movies to be on the bill that you didn't order. Are you sure that someone else in your household didn't order them?"

"There is no one else here. I live alone."

"Do you have a cat?"

"Yes, I have a cat! Now what does that have to do with it?" She was really getting perturbed.

"Well, sometimes cats step on the remote buttons, a movie starts to play and they find it to be entertaining. The next time they get bored, they do it again."

She screamed into the phone, "My damn cat did not order twenty movies!"

"Are you sure?"

"Look, don't give me this crap!" she yelled into the phone.

"Ma'am, you don't have to yell at me. It is not my fault that your cat ordered movies without your permission."

She screamed even louder, "Are you freakin' crazy? My cat did not order movies! Listen, buddy, don't make me come over there! I'll show you…"

"Please hold." There was a click, and the music was playing again.

Lainie was shaking with rage, and laid the phone on the counter. She took a deep breath and shouted, "Midnight, come forth!" Her large black cat came running around the corner and leapt into her arms.

Closing her eyes, she began to chant, "By means of flight, by dark of night, of thee I hear, to bring thou near. If speed be quick, if light be bright, you come to me, to be in sight." She shifted the cat to one arm and made a swirling motion toward the floor in front of her.

There was a hard wind that blew into the room lifting some loose papers into a small whirlwind where she had pointed. Suddenly a man in his mid-twenties with greasy hair, jeans, a short-sleeved white shirt and tie appeared in front of her.

The guy was freaked out to be sure, and he was still in a sitting position when he appeared. He fell to the floor as if someone had pulled the chair out from under him. "What the heck! Where am I?"

"You, sir, are in the house of the cat you believe orders movies, and he would like to show you what he really does when he gets bored!" With that, she swept her arm towards him and he began to shrink down and change form as his clothes became too large and dropped off around him. His nose was growing longer as he shrunk to the size and shape of a medium white rat.

"You see, sir," she pronounced the respectful term with sarcasm. "You never really know who you are talking to when you're on the phone, and this time you chose the wrong person to pick a fight with!" She spoke down at the rat as it shivered on the floor, peeking out from under the white shirt.

"At him, Midnight! And, please, take him outside to the trash when you're finished with him." She smiled as the cat jumped from her arms and chased the rat out of the room. Brushing herself off, she walked to the counter where she had set the phone, and pressed the OFF button. Almost immediately she pressed the ON button and began to re-dial.

Horror Challenge Topic Suggested by:
Heather Badgwell – A Pizza Cutter

KUNG FU PIZZA

From the time he was ten years old, Steve had been considered a scrawny kid. Even now at seventeen, he couldn't seem to gain weight, no matter how hard he tried. At five feet eight inches tall, he was certainly not the kind of guy who people looked up to. His father used to tell him, "You're lucky you are thin. Wait until you are in your thirties, that weight will catch up to you." It had obviously caught up with his dad.

At school, the kids didn't make fun of him for being thin. In fact sometimes he felt invisible from the lack of attention. Other kids who were different got picked on. Someone noticed them at least!

He'd asked for a set of free weights when he began his freshman year. He told his dad he was going to bulk up, but his dad had only laughed. He must have gone to the sporting goods store and bought the weights, however, since Steve found them under the tree when he and his sister woke up that Christmas.

Secretly, he had lifted weights in the basement every day after that. At the end of his workout he would step on the scale, but never a pound of muscle was gained. Bulking up didn't go too well either. Almost no one ever noticed his muscles beneath his loose shirts. He just looked small and scrawny as usual.

In his sophomore year, he fell in love with foreign martial arts films. He figured that adding some martial arts moves to his workout might help him reach his goals. He moved his television and DVD player out of his room and into the basement.

Steve spent hours practicing his moves while watching his DVDs. He fantasized about walking home from school and having an encounter with someone who wanted to start some trouble. After months of practice, he figured he could handle himself but, even then, he was still scrawny Steve and no one took any notice.

Now in his junior year, he got his first real job at Luna Pizza working in the kitchen. He credited his martial arts for helping him to be exceptionally good at tossing the dough for the crust. Everyone who worked with him, including Katie, would take a moment to watch when he was doing it.

He was also pretty talented with the pizza cutter. It was heavy, industrial grade and he would flip it and catch it behind his back between cuts. All in all, he put on quite a show behind the counter in the kitchen. Not that he really cared about putting on a show as much as he hoped to impress Katie. He really wanted to ask her out, but he was so painfully shy, he couldn't muster up the nerve to ask.

One Friday night, the boss had asked him if he could stay until closing. It would be Katie, Josh, Vito, and him. Vito was the boss's nephew and he was always trying to do as little work as possible. He spent most of his time flirting with any attractive female who happened in for a slice – exactly what he was doing the night of the robbery.

Vito was sitting at the counter talking to a woman while Katie was cleaning tables. Steve and Josh were in the kitchen working on a large order when the two hooded thugs came through the door. They brandished their guns and grabbed

Katie straight away. Vito jumped up and had just enough time to say, "Hey, what the..." before they pistol-whipped him and he fell to the floor unconscious.

Steve could see that Katie was being held with a gun to her head. She was crying and begging the guy not to hurt her. Josh freaked out and ran to the cooler to hide inside. That made Steve the last man standing, albeit a young scrawny man.

He had been cutting a pizza with the round wheel cutter and when they ordered him to the register, he gripped the cutter tightly in his hand. "Open the register and give us everything you got!" Steve realized that the thugs weren't wearing any masks. Most likely that meant they had intended to kill all witnesses. With the implications of this running through his mind, Steve snapped.

In the blink of an eye and with a flip of his wrist, he threw the pizza cutter at the guy holding the gun to Katie's head. With a solid 'THUNK" the wheel of the cutter lodged an inch deep in the guy's forehead. The gun fell from his hand and he went to his knees clutching at his face as Katie screamed and ran behind the counter.

The other thug looked at his partner in shock. Steve took the advantage and leapt to the counter top, using it as a springboard as he flew through the air in a Kung Fu pose that would have made Bruce Lee proud. His extended foot impacted the face of the remaining gunmen and shattered his jaw. He fell to the floor with a thud. Steve kicked him repeatedly with enough force to cause him to levitate off the floor. Then dropped him with a punch to the kidney.

The guy with the pizza cutter in his forehead was either dead or unconscious on the floor. The other one was coughing up blood and trying to crawl toward the door.

Steve yelled as loud as he could to the back of the kitchen, "Josh, get your ass out here and dial 911!"

Josh came to the phone to dial as Steve went to Katie who was huddled down on the floor behind the counter. "Are you okay? Did that guy hurt you?" Katie was still shaking and crying and shook her head in response. Relieved, he helped her stand and patted her arm to let her know that everything would be all right now.

Going to the door to lock up the restaurant until the police arrived, he stepped around the guy he'd left on the floor. Just then the injured thug reached out and grabbed him by the ankle. Without looking down. Steve stomped the top of the guy's head slamming it to the floor. He took a few more steps toward the door when he stopped and turned around toward Katie.

"Hey, Katie," he waited for her to look up. "I don't know about you, but I'm quitting this dumb job... " He hesitated a moment then finished his thought. "Uh, there's a dance next week after the game and I was wondering if you might go with me?"

Without saying a word, she nodded. Steve turned and smiled as he went to lock the door.

Horror Challenge Topic Suggested by:
Maria M. – Shampoo

BAD HAIR DAY

After her divorce was final, Lauren spent weeks at home alone asking herself what had gone wrong. The day finally came when she realized that both she and her husband had contributed to the failure of their marriage. She laid the matter to rest and, that Saturday morning she was ready to start living again.

She made a plan to head down to the village by the University where the cool shops and little cafés were plentiful. She enjoyed a light lunch before taking a walk around, popping in and out of the shops. One very intriguing shop hung a simple sign that said Magick. It was hand painted in bright inviting colors and Lauren felt compelled to stop in and see all the unique things they might have there.

She was expecting a shop where kits and tricks for magicians were sold. Instead there was a strange and delightful mix of candles, scents, jewelry, clothes and other things that might grab the attention of a young college girl. The shopkeeper came in from the back when the bell had rung on the door.

The older woman had long gray hair pulled back with a headband, however her face looked much younger than Lauren had guessed at first glance. She was dressed in a long, flowing, flowered dress that reminded Lauren of her hippy chick days some 25 years earlier.

"Hello." She nearly sang as she greeted her customer. "Feel free to look around. I'll have a nice suggestion for you in a few moments."

Lauren thought that a strange comment, but the woman seemed sincere so she took her time looking at jewelry and dresses, soaps and incense. There was so much to see, but there just didn't seem to be anything that she couldn't live without. The woman watched her all the while, smiling sweetly until Lauren looked at her directly and finally made eye contact.

"You are ready then," the shopkeeper said quite matter-of-factly. "You are not attracted to any of these things because you are a passionate woman who has just lost a great love." She was smiling as she spoke. "Yes?"

"Yes, but how did you know..."

"It is in your aura. The ripples are clear, you see. You need something to help you on your way to a new and exciting time of your life. Come with me dear." She motioned toward a beaded curtain that separated the main shop from a smaller room. As Lauren followed her through the curtain, she felt the hairs on the back of her neck standing up.

"I had a strange feeling as we entered this room," she said, rubbing her neck.

"Indeed you did. This room is for special customers only!" The woman was beaming. "And you, my dear, are very special indeed. Please take a moment to look carefully before you decide. Most of what you see here could be yours today, but I must tell you that for your first visit we should start with something simple."

Lauren read the names of the items on the handwritten labels of the beautiful colored jars that filled one of the three-tiered shelves. They had romantic names such as Love,

Attraction, Lust, Just a Little, and Immersed. She picked up one of the bottles and looked at the liquid inside. "Are these perfumes?" she turned to ask.

The woman smiled broadly. "Oh no, my dear. They are potions exactly as labeled. I would suggest we start with something less complicated. Try the soaps and lotions today and, if you like them, you can always come back for the more potent of potions. Like they say, start small and work your way up."

Lauren must have spent a half hour looking. Taking the woman at her word, she considered the labels more seriously. She chose something that might be 'safe' for experimentation. It was a bottle of mint and chamomile shampoo, one of the few items that actually had a primitive printed label.

Along with the words, "Mint and Chamomile Shampoo," the label declared that using it "Brings life and body to dull and lifeless hair." On the back, there were directions. "Pour an amount no more than the hollow of your palm. Lather, Rinse and Repeat." Simple enough. She paid the woman, thanking her for her special attention, and then found herself hurrying home to try this strange product.

She was nearly giddy with excitement as she stepped into the shower. She poured the recommended amount into her palm, massaging it into her scalp and squeezing it through her long brown hair. Her skin was cooled by the mint, and she felt invigorated as she rinsed her hair. When she was finished, she wrapped it in a towel and stepped up to the mirror to apply some face cream and check for stray whiskers that often plagued her face in this stage of her life.

Leaning close to the mirror, she felt movement inside of her towel. It was just a wiggle at first, then something jerked. She was afraid to look to see what might be the cause. Had a mouse crawled onto her towel when she wasn't looking? She was horrified at the thought. She stood watching the towel in the mirror as it moved again on her head. It definitely was not a mouse, but it could be something else inside the towel.

Pushing down her fears, she tilted her head forward and pulled the towel off as quickly as she could. Bringing her head up again, she looked into the mirror and let out a shriek. Her hair was sticking straight up as though she were holding it, forming a point at its ends. She thought she was hallucinating as it started to move. Almost like a snake, it danced on the top of her head, morphing into the shape of a perfectly formed woman's body. It moved on her head like a belly dancer, as she stood frozen with fear.

Carefully, Lauren reached up and grabbed it. The belly dancing hair felt solid and continued to dance even as she gripped it in her hand. What in the world was this? It was not her imagination. This thing was real!

Just then, she remembered what the woman in the shop had said. "They are potions and exactly as labeled." She ran to the shower and grabbed the bottle as her hair began whipping around into a spiral. The label read, "Lather, Rinse and Repeat," and she had forgotten to repeat!

Without hesitation, Lauren turned on the water and jumped into the shower. She hurriedly squeezed the correct amount of shampoo into her palm and attempted to put it on her hair only to find that it had formed itself into a hand and was trying to stop her. Reaching up with her other hand, she felt her hair grab hold of her wrist. Quickly she applied the shampoo using her free hand.

She did as best she could, while her hair seemed determined to stop her. Lathering it in, the hair gradually ceased its struggle and succumbed to the magic ingredients as she began to rinse the shampoo out. A half hour later, she was standing in front of the mirror again admiring her shiny, full-bodied perfect hair. It really had worked the way it promised!

Early the next morning, the woman walked up to her shop to open for the day. She smiled as she recognized her customer from the previous day. "I'm ready to try some of the finer things in life," the happy customer said as the woman unlocked the door and stepped inside. Switching on the light, the shopkeeper turned and smiled again at her customer, "Indeed you are, my dear. Indeed you are."

Horror Challenge Topic Suggested by:
Lynn Worton – Bus Stop

ONE GREEN BALLOON

The boy was sitting at the bus stop with his baseball cap and a green balloon. He was relishing what appeared to be a Tootsie Pop when Anthony sat down next to him. He didn't seem to mind that Anthony had joined him there. In fact, he just sat and watched his balloon as it floated above his head.

This was an important day for Anthony. He had worked at the firm for nine years now and today he would learn whether he had won the promotion he had been competing for. If he were selected, it wouldn't mean much in the way of a pay increase, but the prestige that came along with the job meant that he was on his way up.

While he was waiting, he daydreamed about how he had started as a security guard and caught the attention of one of the board members. The man had leveraged his influence to move Anthony into the sales department where every day he out performed his peers. Since then, he had worked into management and still maintained residual sales that totaled more than his three best sellers combined.

Not only had he done well for himself, he had done well enough after three years to have the security to start his family. His son was just about the age of the boy sitting next to him and his wife was pregnant with their second child

He looked at his watch to see if the bus was overdue, but it would only be another minute or so before it was scheduled to come by. "That candy must be pretty good," he said to the boy. "Are you waiting for your mom to come out of the store?"

The boy shook his head and swung his legs back and forth under the bench. Anthony looked around to see if there were some other adult nearby, but there was no one else on the sidewalk.

"Are you on your way to school?" He tried again, but again the boy shook his head and bit into his candy with a crunch.

Anthony felt concern now. Didn't this boy's parents understand how dangerous it was to leave a child on a park bench in the inner city these days? As he pondered the situation, he considered calling the police. Maybe the boy was abandoned. Even though he didn't look upset, it was possible. So he asked a more pointed question. "Are you waiting for someone?"

This time, the boy looked at him and pointed straight at him and smiled. Now, that sent a shiver up Anthony's spine. Why would this kid be waiting for him of all people? He tried to shed the creepy feeling, to think of something else, but this had pushed his thoughts about the promotion to the back of his mind. He thought again about calling the police and pulled his phone from his pocket.

Just then he heard the bus coming down the street. Rather than make the call, he put the phone back in his pocket. When the bus was about a block away, the boy dropped his lollipop. He bent to pick it up, but then the green balloon slipped from his fingers and drifted toward the street.

In the blink of an eye, the boy was up and after it. Anthony could see what was about to happen. He jumped up and ran after the boy to prevent him from stepping in front of the bus. The bus was very near as he lunged toward the street. The boy and the balloon disappeared in front of him. As much as he tried to stop his momentum, he tripped and fell into the gutter two seconds before the bus rolled up and over him.

Anthony was crushed under the wheels as the bus came to a stop. The driver realized what had happened and put the bus in reverse, backing up a few yards. He got off the bus to see if there was anything he could do to help the poor man who had fallen in front of it.

"Oh my God, Oh my God!" the driver repeated as a few people wandered over to see what had happened. Anthony lay close to the gutter, his body nearly cut in two from the weight of the bus. The distraught driver sat on the bench in shock as one of the passengers used their phone to call the police. As they awaited the arrival of emergency services, no one seemed to notice the boy with the green balloon who had sat down next to the driver.

When the police later notified his family, his wife was overcome in her grief and sat at the table crying for hours. In the tavern down the street from the bus stop, the six o'clock local news was on the television as usual. The report of the accident was merely a blip on the screen. "A local man was killed today in a tragic bus accident near the intersection of Fifth and Elm. Ironically, it is the same location where six-year old Michael Lester died in a similar accident just one year ago today. A police investigation has ruled out foul play and the next of kin have been notified."

Horror Challenge Topic Suggested by:
Samantha Moody – Deck of Playing Cards

THE REAL DEAL

Clive was sitting at the bar sipping his drink when a stranger sat down on the barstool next to him. He really didn't feel like talking to anyone so he didn't pay attention to the guy until he slapped a deck of cards on the counter.

"Hey, buddy, I bet you a drink that I can take these cards right here, let you pick one, and guess the one you picked."

Clive turned his head slowly and looked at the man. "What?"

The stranger was smiling at him. "You know, it's a card trick. I let you pick a card then you put it back in the deck. I shuffle then pull your card from the deck." He hesitated, waiting for a response before continuing. "I bet you a drink I'll get it right."

"Anybody can do that one." Clive thought he was being sly by requesting, "Do something really fancy and I'll buy you that drink."

"Tell me what you consider 'fancy'"

"Well, how about the one where I take a card and write my name on it. I give it to you, and you put it back in the deck. Then you shuffle the cards and choose one. When you show it to me, it's my card. Then you tear it up and eat it, before reaching in my pocket to pull out a card that's mine with my writing on it."

The stranger just sat there glaring at him, before speaking. "Do I look like David Freakin' Copperfield to you?"

Clive laughed. "No, but if you expect to win a drink, you'll have to do better than the lame trick you suggested."

"Lame, huh? You want to go all in, then?"

Clive was curious. "What's 'all in' the way you see it?"

"If I do something really intense, I mean really freaky, you give me all the cash you have on you. How much do you have?"

Clive reached in his pocket and pulled out his money clip and flipped through the bills. "I have about a hundred and fifty. But, what if I'm not impressed, what do I win?"

"Oh, no problem. I have at least that much on me. We'll go one on one. Cool?"

"Sure." Clive replied and held out his hand. "Shake on it?"

The man shook his hand. He opened the box of cards and shuffled them. Fanning out the cards, he said, "Pick any card and hold it."

Clive chose a card and held it while the man reached into his pocket and pulled out a thin permanent marker. He handed it to Clive and said, "Go ahead and write your name on it, then put it back in the deck."

Clive looked down at his card. It was a five of clubs. He took the cap off the marker and wrote his name. He replaced the cap and laid the marker on the counter. The man was still holding the fanned out cards, so he slid his back into the deck.

The man proceeded to shuffle the cards and then, unexpectedly, he put the deck back in the box. "Aren't you even going to try to find the card? Giving up so fast?"

"Oh no, not giving up. I'm going to need both hands for the next part." He was smiling confidently as he slid the deck into his pocket. "Okay, now stand up. I need to get in close for this."

Clive obliged and stood next to the stool. The stranger looked around as he moved in closer. He put one hand on the back of Clive's neck and the fingers of his other hand bunched tightly together against his stomach. Then, before Clive could react or move away, the man thrust his hand forward through shirt and skin, burying it wrist deep.

Clive's eyes widened and he let out a gasp as the stranger's hand entered his stomach, and quickly pulled back out. It was wet but showed no signs of blood. Clive experienced the oddest sensation as the hole in his abdomen closed back up, and he began to cough and choke. He felt as though he were going to pass out.

The stranger moved to his side and began slapping Clive on the back as he coughed. He came around to face Clive and instructed him to open his mouth. Clive felt as if he were dying and hoped the man could help him, and so complied.

The smiling man shoved his hand into Clive's mouth and halfway down his throat. Twisting his wrist as he pulled it out, his hand emerged with a playing card clenched between the fingers.

He waited for Clive to regain his composure, all the while holding the card in his hand. When Clive stopped coughing, the stranger held the card up so Clive could see it. It was the five of clubs with Clive's handwriting and bits of the sandwich he had eaten half an hour earlier.

"Holy shit! How'd you do that?" he asked.

The man laid the card on the counter and wiped his hand with a napkin. "Well, like I said, I'm not Copperfield. He's just an illusionist. My shit's real." He turned and started to walk away.

Clive yelled after him, "What about the money?"

As the guy pushed open the door to the street, he pulled Clive's money clip out of his pocket and yelled over his shoulder, "We're straight!"

Suggested by J.H. Glaze
A Bonus Story for Volume I

DAMSEL IN DISTRESS

Jack had been at the bar for hours and needed to head home to sleep off his buzz before going to work in the morning. As he walked across the parking lot toward his car, he fumbled around in his pocket for his keys and ended up dropping them beside a pickup truck. It was one of those trucks that had been half jacked up to simulate a monster truck, and it sat high off the ground.

When he bent over to retrieve the keys, he could have sworn he saw a woman lying on the ground on the other side. He decided to step around the truck to investigate. What he saw made his adrenaline surge and sobered him enough to evaluate the situation.

There was a woman lying on the ground, sure enough, face down on the pavement. She had long blond hair, and her leather mini skirt didn't offer much cover for her shapely legs as they kicked against the ground.

The man standing next to her in a dark suit had one foot planted firmly on the back of her neck. He was speaking some kind of foreign language as he held her to the ground. She, in turn, was spouting muffled profanities as he spoke.

Jack was never one to allow such actions to go unchallenged. He yelled at the man, "Hey you! Asshole! Take your foot off her. Let her up!"

The man turned to look at him with fire in his eyes and replied, "Look, you better mind your own business and move along." He turned back to the woman and continued with his rant.

Jack was not about to let this continue. He decided rather than argue with the man, he would pull out the small handgun he carried in the back of his jeans. He didn't feel like having a conversation at the moment, and this would be over in a minute if he maintained his nerve.

He reached around and pulled the piece from its holster and then aimed it at the strange man as he gave his warning. "Look, buddy. I don't want any trouble. Just let the woman get up and leave so we can both go home and sleep it off."

The man glared at him and replied, "Sir, you must not intervene. This demon would sooner eviscerate you than discuss your heroics. You must move along now and allow me to dispatch this beast."

Jack felt the last of his drunken patience fade as he ordered, "Either step away from the bitch, or I'm putting a slug in the side of your head! I'm gonna count to three." At which point he began his count, "One..."

"Sir, you shall regret this folly."

"Two..."

"This is no woman, my friend."

"Thr..."

"You win sir. Please allow me to step back, and I shall allow this devil to retreat in any direction it likes."

Jack was relieved that the man was cooperating. He had begun to be concerned that he would have to shoot him. "Okay," Jack said. "Step back."

As the man removed his foot from the woman's neck, Jack could have sworn that he heard loud growling as from a dog. In a single fluid movement, she was suddenly to her feet and running straight at him. Her mouth was open wide, wider than any human mouth could open. He could see rows of long sharp teeth as she went straight for his gut.

Before he could react, she swung her arm at him. Her fingers were tipped with claws like a jungle cat and ripped a large patch of his shirt away along with the flesh beneath it. As his entrails fell at his feet, he began to black out. By the time he hit the ground he was over the edge of the abyss and into the darkness. As the spark of his life burned out, he heard the stranger mutter as he walked away. "Ignorant, arrogant humans!"

Horror Challenge Topics Suggested by:
Cory Fipps – Dumas
M.J Schutte – Black Panther

SLIP OF THE TONGUE

On the morning of July 4th, Dumas, Texas was gone. The town of about 14,000 people had been there at midnight the night before when Roberto left his lover's house with the excuse that he had to go home and get some sleep so he could function at work the next day.

Carl finished his shift at the Moore County Airport at 4:00 a.m. and slogged his way to his car to head home. He was dreaming about a few cold beers to wash away the stress of his long day. When he reached the town limits on State Highway 87, he was surprised to find the concrete of the highway ending abruptly in a field. There was no escaping the obvious. There were no buildings as far as he could see. Even the grain elevators were gone.

Cheryl had been visiting her mother in Lubbock after she and Hank had gotten into a big fight. She had taken the kids and left like she always did, giving him time to cool down. Driving back home that morning, she too found herself stopping her car as the road came to an end in a field.

Every person who had been outside the town limits that morning and tried to return home the next day found there was no home to return to. They could find no sign that a town had ever existed except for the highways and roads that came to an end in a large open area.

Inside the town limits another story was unfolding.

It was 3:00 a.m. when Elizabeth had begun her incantation. Her intent was to have revenge on the people in town for the persecution they had visited upon her these past few months. Alone in her small trailer across from the park, she began weaving her spell.

The ingredients she needed were gathered from the yards of the townsfolk. She took flowers from gardens, children's toys from driveways, something from the store and other items she gathered around the perimeter of the town. She stirred the items together in a very large pot of water on her gas stove. The final ingredient was the image of the town she had cut from an Atlas map and neatly trimmed along the dotted border. She dropped it in and stirred it into the mixture.

Her spell book had been obtained five years earlier from a rundown bookstore before she had moved here. She had performed many smaller spells from it with great success, but this one was more complex. The result she sought included misfortune and suffering, including skin irritation and lesions for the people of the town.

Elizabeth thought it should last at least three days if she executed it correctly, but that night she had broken her reading glasses and as she recited the words, she had misspoken a few without realizing she had done so. When she removed the lid from the pot, the steam should have covered the town in a fog in order to spread the curse. Instead, as the lid was lifted, a vortex spiraled upward and out of it.

Immediately, her trailer blew to pieces, and she could only stare in horror as the vortex grew and continued down the road to the edge of town. Once there, the vortex spread as a wall of wind that blew from the edge of town to the center. The swirling wind was steady for about ten minutes before it stopped.

Her neighbors thought a twister was coming and hunkered down in their trailers until the howling of the wind was silenced, but shortly afterward they came pouring out into the darkness with flashlights to see what had happened. What they found was Liz, standing on the exposed floor of her trailer with bits of debris scattered on the ground surrounding her. No wall was left standing nor one bit of the trailer, save for the floor and the wheels beneath the frame that supported it.

Of course, they asked her what had happened, but Elizabeth pretended not to know. Somehow they knew that they had survived more than your typical storm. The first clue was the lack of damage to anything but Elizabeth's home. Then there was the total absence of light. There were no streetlights shining, no lights from homes or cars. There was no moonlight and even the billions of stars that would normally be visible on a clear night had disappeared. Dumas didn't seem to be in Texas anymore. It didn't seem to be anywhere.

Meanwhile, that afternoon at the edge of the empty field where once was the town, traffic was backed up for miles on the various arteries leading into town. Delivery trucks, people passing through, and people coming to visit families or on business all found the same empty field. Some responded to this discovery with sobbing and some with plain old head scratching. There was simply no explanation for it.

As the day dragged on, tents began to appear along the edge. Many were occupied by loved ones who refused to believe their families and friends had simply disappeared.

They vowed to wait for the town to return, fully expecting that somehow it would.

Earlier, the people remaining within the border of Dumas found there would be no sunrise and no change to their situation. They walked the streets and eventually headed toward the Square where everything and anything important happened. It was where the Christmas concert was held each winter and would be the location of the 4th of July festival that night. On this day of darkness, no one was leading the way. The people simply gathered together and stood waiting there for guidance. That is when the creatures of darkness came.

Like black panthers in the night, with massive fangs and claws and on padded feet obscured by darkness, they silently surrounded the people in the square. In one accord, they descended upon the townsfolk without notice. Flashlights fell from hands as the victims were pulled to the ground screaming and consumed in a single bite by gigantic creatures, ancient and overpowering, never before known to man.

Those who had remained inside their homes for protection sat in candlelight waiting to be rescued after the strange storm. They were horrified as the doors and walls of their homes were crashed to splinters by ravenous beasts seeking their prey. There was nowhere to run and nowhere to hide.

Elizabeth had sought shelter from one of her kind neighbors whose husband had passed months earlier. She could hear the screams of the dying, the men, women, and children who had taunted her these many months. It was heart wrenching to realize that those she had meant to simply punish for a few days were dying in horror all around her.

As the creatures moved on the trailer court, the crashing and screaming grew louder. Elizabeth peeked through the curtains trying to see what was creating the carnage, but she could only see shadows moving before the side of a trailer would be torn away and the person dragged into the small yard beside it. In the midst of the shrieks, the person seemed to just disappear into the darkness.

The trailer she was hiding in was next!

She heard movement at the rear of the trailer then at the front. Her neighbor was trying to fit under the table when the wall beside her was torn away by huge claws and the woman looked at her with hopeless eyes full of terror as she tried to scream for help, and then she was gone. Elizabeth closed her eyes and waited to be taken, but instead she listened as the shadowy creatures moved away.

Suddenly she remembered why they would spare her. She had added protection for herself to the incantation. She was not supposed to suffer the torment she had planned for the rest of the town. The tears streamed down her cheeks as she realized what hell she had brought to these people. They had never really done anything to cause her pain but stare and talk behind her back. Sometimes there was snickering, but nothing for them to deserve this.

She determined to follow the beasts, not by sight, but by the sounds of their breathing and chewing of victims that they seemed to cough up and eat again as they searched for the next one. She pleaded with them to stop, to leave and not return, but the demonic creatures seemed not to notice.

For two days the mayhem continued until the last living being had been located and consumed. On the third night, at exactly 3:00 a.m., the stars suddenly returned to the sky as the town returned to its place. Like a puzzle piece, it was laid down just so, and each road reconnected with proper alignment.

The people who had been occupying the edge of town tried to move in from their place of vigil, but the State Police and the National Guard held the barricade tight until someone could investigate what had happened. Men in hazard suits that covered them completely went into the town, and after an hour returned visibly shaken. Not one would speak about what they had found and reinforcements were called in to keep the people out. A wave of anger spread through the crowd and only the threat of the armed soldiers stopped them from rioting and rushing the town.

Hours after the town reappeared, a woman came walking toward the barricade from the main street of the town. Her hair was completely white and she seemed dazed as she was accosted at the barricade and led to one of the large tents that had been erected. The doctors tried to speak to her, but it was obvious that some great trauma had rendered her mentally unstable.

As they loaded her into an ambulance, she kept repeating the same thing over and over. "Two words, two words! The fatal difference between what I said and what I meant to say. It was caused by two misspoken words. It was only two words, two words!"

Horror Challenge Topic Suggested by:
Jenny Needham – Monkeys

MUST. HAVE. STONE.

How can you tell when a major event is about to change your life, especially when it happens in the most innocuous way? What if you don't even recognize that anything has changed until some disastrous event has occurred because of you?

Ron was a collector. I know, your imagination can run wild with that one, but he was, nonetheless, a collector of small, smooth stones. For a collector, he wasn't too concerned whether the stones were precious or not. He didn't need rubies or emeralds or the like. He simply enjoyed collecting nice smooth stones.

As he walked down the street, wherever he might be, he would spot a stone that fit his requirement and stop to pick it up. He would hold it in the palm of his hand and bounce it there to get a feel for its size and weight. Then he'd roll it around in his fingers to test the smoothness before deciding if it was worthy of his collection.

Ron could be considered a thief since most of these desirable stones were often found in the landscape in front of the homes he passed by. He had most likely pilfered the orderly landscaped beds of hundreds, if not thousands of homeowners these many years. Perhaps if Ron had sought help for his affliction, he may have been diagnosed with some level of obsessive-compulsive disorder but, in laymen's terms, he was simply a petty rock thief.

On this particular sunny day as he walked down the street and picked up yet another stone, he simply put it in his pocket and went on his way. As he passed the Mini Mart, he decided to stop in for a drink. He walked through the door and straight toward the coolers in the back of the store. Seconds later the door closed behind him and the little string of bells hanging from it gave a cheerful ring.

He stood in front of the coolers looking at the displays full of bottles, but he could not find what he was looking for, a bottle of cold Mocha Cappuccino. They carried the regular coffee and caramel flavor, but no Mocha. Disappointed, Ron grabbed a cola instead of a coffee drink. "You'd think they'd have a cooler full of Mocha flavor instead of the other crap," he grumbled. He heard a noise behind him, but didn't pay any attention as he walked toward the front of the store.

When he reached the counter, he waited for the cashier to ring up his purchase, but the cashier seemed in a daze, staring toward the back of the store. "How much?" he finally asked the young woman behind the counter.

"Huh?" she said. "Oh, two dollars."

He pulled two dollars from his wallet, laid them on the counter and walked out. There wasn't any need to wait for a receipt. Outside the store, he shook his head and thought to himself, "I hate it when they get the young girls to work the register. They're always off in their own little world. They should get that old guy back. At least he was always right on top of things."

The minute Ron walked out the door, the girl went back to get a better look at the cooler. From the counter it looked as though all the bottles in it had changed to Mocha Cappuccino. Before she could reach the glass doors, she vanished. In her place stood an old man in a suit, who immediately fell face first to the floor landing with a thud.

Ron hadn't heard that the old man who once worked at the store had passed away two weeks earlier, but now his corpse was lying on the floor in front of the cooler for the next customer to discover. He was two blocks away when a woman found the body, her screams were far out of range of Ron's hearing.

Did I mention that Ron was on his way to work on that sunny morning? Well, he arrived about one minute before start time. He walked straight to his desk, turned on his computer, and began to sort the papers on his desk. He liked to put them in order of priority. After a minute or so, the login screen popped up. It required a password change – again. "Why do I have to change my password so often?" he complained, dropping one of the papers in his hand. "I should be able to log in without a password." He bent over to pick up the paper.

When he sat up and looked at the screen, the login message was gone and the computer was going through it's regular setup routine. "Huh? That's weird. Maybe they changed something." He waited until he had a desktop full of icons before opening his email client.

Ron worked steadily throughout the morning, taking care of the business at hand. He might be a lot of things, including an obsessed rock thief, but he was certainly dedicated to his job. In fact, he was so busy that morning that it was three minutes into his coffee break before he noticed the time.

Richard was already in the break room when Ron got there. Typically, he went in early to get the coffee going, and no one complained if he took an extra ten minutes to do so as long as the coffee was ready. Today, however, there was no coffee prepared and Richard was talking on his phone. "Yeah, baby, I understand, but I told you we can't afford to go on a cruise. We'll just have to make some other arrangements." He was silent while the person on the other end was speaking, and replied, "Well, it's break time so we'll talk about this later, okay?" Richard pursed his lips as he ended the call.

"Everything cool there, Rick?" Ron asked him.

"Not really. My wife is upset because we can't go on the cruise I promised her for our anniversary. I just don't have the cash right now, not after getting braces for Amy."

"I hear ya." Ron was sympathetic. He added, "You never know. Something could change. Maybe you have a lottery ticket in your wallet you forgot about and it's a big winner."

"Man, that reminds me. I do have a lottery ticket in my wallet I forgot about. I should go and check it online to see if I won." He was already hurrying out of the room.

Ron started to make some coffee. A few minutes later, Michael sauntered in. "Any coffee left?"

"Yeah, Mike, as soon as we make some," replied Ron as he poured water into the coffee maker. "Ricardo was busy with his lady on the phone and forgot to make it."

"That's why I like you man. You always take care of business." Mike sat at the small table to wait. "Look, I was talking to my wife last night about the house and she wants me to do some work on the roof…"

Just then they heard a loud yell coming from the office. Alaina was just coming through the door smiling. Mike asked, "So what's going on out there?"

"I was finishing up a presentation when Rick came back to his desk mumbling something about a lottery ticket he was going to check online. Two seconds later, he found out he'd won five million bucks! Turns out he had the ticket in his wallet for some time. Some people are just lucky, I guess."

Ron was stunned. "That's really weird. I was just joking when I told him he might have a winning ticket, and he goes in there and finds out it really is a big winner."

"That's kinda freaky, isn't it?" Mike was pouring a cup of coffee and poured one for Ron. "Here dude, drink up. Us losers have to go back to work." He handed the coffee over, and headed back to his desk.

Ron sat there for a minute sipping his coffee, and then headed back to his desk. When he past Mike's cubicle, he found him already back to work. "So, what do you think about the chances?" He nodded over to Richard who was already cleaning out his desk. "I think he's quitting right now."

"I would too! Wouldn't you?"

"Yeah, I guess so." Ron turned away and went back to his desk. About a half hour later, he felt movement behind him and turned around to find Mike standing there. "Hey, Ron, before we were interrupted by Mister Lucky, I was going to tell you... well, ask you..."

"Yeah, say it." Ron was sitting there looking at his friend as he tried to spit out the question.

"Well, my wife wants me to go up on the roof this weekend and put in a vent, you know, to draw out the heat in the summer?"

"Wow, that sucks. I feel for ya." Ron was sincere.

"Yeah, well, I was wondering... if you aren't doing anything Saturday, maybe you could come over and help me?"

Ron looked at him for a long moment before answering. "Dude, I'm totally afraid of heights. I don't think so."

Mike pleaded with him, "Please, Ron. I can't do it myself. I need an extra pair of hands."

"I'll make you a deal, buddy." Ron was trying to figure out a nice way to say no.

"Yeah, sure." Ron said the first thing that came to his mind.

"I'll tell you what. I'll come over and help you on your roof ... when monkeys fly out of my ass!" He leaned back in his chair and let his laughter soften the blow.

Mike looked disappointed, and Ron began squirming in his seat.

"Ow! Shit!" Ron jumped out of his chair clutching at his backside. He was clearly in pain and his pants, loose fitting as usual, were swelling in the back. "What the hell?" In sheer desperation, he unfastened his belt, unbuttoned his pants, and pulled the back out to make more room. As soon as he did, a real live little monkey with wings flew out of his pants and across the office. Right behind it was another, then another, and before Ron could say a word, there were half dozen flying monkeys bouncing off the walls and trying to escape through closed windows.

Ron was hopping up and down, yelling and flapping the back of his pants in and out until the monkeys were all free. In the process, the smooth stone he had picked up earlier dropped from his pocket and rolled under a nearby desk. Women were screaming while everyone was ducking for cover. Finally one of the guys managed to open a window. The strange flying monkeys flew out, one after another, and just like that, they were gone.

Ron was stunned and bleeding from several bites he had received while the critters were trapped in his pants. He could not explain what had just happened. After a brief conversation with the boss, he went home for the day.

Saturday morning around 8:00 a.m., there was a knock at Mike's door. He was taken by surprise to find Ron standing there with a stepladder. "Hey, buddy, you feeling all right? You left in a hurry after that monkey thing the other day." He was concerned about his friend despite the comedy of the experience in hindsight.

"Yeah, I'm fine. I have to tell you, that was the weirdest shit I ever experienced." They both started laughing at the pun and, after they laughed it out, Ron finished what he had to say. "Anyway, a deal is a deal, and I'm here to help you with the roof."

Horror Challenge Topic Suggested by:
Amanda Wimer - a song

THIRTEEN CORPSES

The Great Depression of the early Twentieth Century
stretched on for years and drove many good people to
desperate acts as they fought for survival amid crushing
unemployment and poverty. Granted, it was not only the
good people who suffered through this time. There was
enough suffering to go around and equally affected the truly
evil. It was those individuals who sometimes turned to
dastardly deeds to keep the engines of their personal
economy running. Jebediah and Lloyd were two such people.

It wasn't like the two of them sat around a campfire one
night and reviewed possible entrepreneurial endeavors in
order to choose from the list. Oh, no, they discovered the
value of a fresh grave early that spring when a gully washer
of a flood unearthed the grave of one of the dearly departed
at the local cemetery.

The coffin that popped out of the ground that day
contained the remains of a woman of modest means, but she
had been buried in her finest clothes and jewelry. As they
lifted the lid of the box, they found her in her finery and
proceeded to liberate her of any item of value.

Having found a new means of revenue, they set out on
the road moving from town to town – present day
"archeologists" they called themselves – recovering lost
treasures from the past. It was too bad that their definition
of the past included anyone who had been unfortunate

enough to be buried mere hours before they happened upon the fresh grave.

So on this moonless night, they had planned for an excavation of the highest order at the Waterton Public Cemetery to be carried out shortly after sunset. As the sun dipped low behind the hills, they waited at the edge of the cemetery sharing a can of Spam lunchmeat and a half loaf of bread.

After an hour or so, Jeb hoisted his shovel to his shoulder and announced, "Lloyd, it is time to ply our trade and see what the dear departed souls have carried to their final resting place for us to find."

Lloyd was a man of few words since the time he had gotten into a fight with a hobo on the train. A single surprise blow to his jaw had caused his friend to bite his tongue half off. Actually Jeb was glad to have a silent partner. Not only did it allow for a more serene life but also, when Lloyd actually did try to speak, the words that came from his mouth were so garbled that Jeb couldn't understand him anyway.

On this night Jeb was in an exceptionally chipper mood, and he began singing a song he had made up weeks before.

"Thirteen corpses buried in a line,
You dig yers up an' I'll dig mine,
When we're both finished
We'll split up all the loot,
Unless the coppers come,
And chase us while they shoot.
OH-h-h!
Thirteen corpses lying on the grass,
Their jewelry and their gold teeth
Pried from their rotting ass."

With that he stopped singing and chuckled as he came to a fresh gravesite. "Hey, Lloyd! How'd you like the new line in the song? I think it works better than the other one."

"Miff da I uk." Lloyd replied.

Jeb just looked at him. "Never mind, Buddy. I should have known better than to ask. Let's get to work."

He pointed out another fresh mound a few feet away and, while Lloyd moved his appointed site, Jeb started digging. He threw shovel after shovel full of dirt over his shoulder in great anticipation as to what their haul could be tonight. Maybe a nice gold pocket watch, or a string of pearls would be there for the taking. However, it was likely they might find nothing at all as most people had sold much of their valuables after these many years of hard times.

An hour passed before Jeb's shovel struck wood. As quickly as he could, he scraped the dirt away from the lid. From his position, all he could see of Lloyd was an occasional shovel full of dirt being tossed out of the hole he was digging. He decided to let the guy dig and see for himself what he had unearthed.

He shoved the edge of the shovel against the crack between the casket and the lid and pushed hard. He pushed down on the handle and gave it all he had. At last, the lid broke free of the nails that held it shut. Jeb bent down and yanked up on the lid swinging it open. He pulled his prized Zippo lighter from his pocket, a "gift" from a recent dig. He flicked the flint wheel with his thumb and the wick burst into yellow flame.

"Shit!" he exclaimed when he saw that the box was empty. There was not even the tiniest fragment of a body in it. He leaned in to look closer and saw a large round hole in the bottom that looked as if it went deep into the ground. "Hey, Lloyd! Come here and look at this!"

Lloyd was nearly finished uncovering the casket in his hole, but he dropped his shovel and climbed up to walk over to find his partner standing about five feet down in an empty coffin. "Hmmm, wha a uck?"

"Yeah, I'd say! Where do you think that hole goes? Maybe there's a tunnel down there. Ya know, like those ones they say are in France? Maybe there's stacks of bodies down there all drippin with gold and jewels." He looked at his friend who had a blank look on his face. "I think I should at least take a look, don't you?"

Lloyd shrugged his shoulders.

"Jump down here and help me." He moved to give the guy enough room to get down in the coffin with him, and Lloyd jumped in.

"I think you should hold my feet while I crawl in there, just in case it's real deep. If it is, you just pull me back out, right?" Lloyd nodded his agreement as Jeb got down on his knees. Before going down into the hole, he measured it with his hands to make sure it was wide enough for him. When he was satisfied, he lay on his stomach and pushed himself to the edge. "Okay. Now, grab my feet. If I yell, pull me back up. Got it?"

Lloyd nodded, grabbed his feet as directed and Jeb started down the hole. At first, he was met with a rush of air that hit him in the face and extinguished his lighter. The air smelled like rotting flesh and quite rank, but instead of concern, he felt even more excited. There must be something down here all right, he thought. He re-lit the lighter and held it out in front of him again. What happened next was beyond all expectation.

Something came rushing up at him from the darkness below. He had crawled down in as far as his knees at this point but instead of yelling for Lloyd to pull him out as they had planned, he screamed, "ARGHHHH!"

Startled, Lloyd jumped and lost his grip on Jeb, who slipped completely into the hole. Bending over to see how far his friend had fallen, he couldn't see a thing. He stepped back up and looked around for something he could burn for light as he felt for the box of matches in his pocket.

As Lloyd was distracted, Jeb's body shot up out of the hole and five feet into the air with his legs kicking. From the waist down to his head, he was half swallowed by something resembling a giant earthworm. It barely made a sound as Jeb's screams were absorbed in the gullet of the monster. If not for the flailing legs kicking him in the back, Lloyd might not have turned around in time to notice what was happening to his friend.

Scared out of his wits, Lloyd screamed as he backed up to the wall of earth surrounding the casket and, still facing the monster, tried to scramble up backwards toward the surface. Meanwhile, the creature lurched upward and swallowed more of Jeb, gulping him down to just below his kneecaps. Lloyd watched in horror as it began to pull itself back into the ground taking his friend with it.

As suddenly as it had appeared, it was gone.

Scared witless, Lloyd scrambled up to the grassy surface and ran, leaving the shovels and his friend behind. He raced back to the railroad tracks where he hid until he could hop the first train to come along.

Later, when the economy started to turn around, Lloyd took a job in a factory. Because he couldn't speak or write, the only way he could express what had happened that night was by drawing pictures. Unfortunately, he wasn't much of an artist either, so no one could tell what the pictures actually meant. Perhaps no one would have believed it if they could.

Lloyd worked in that factory until he died ten years later. When the day came to dispose of his remains, his last will and testament was found in a metal case in his pocket. A simple request, it consisted of two pictures drawn on a sheet of paper. One was a picture of a coffin in a hole in the ground with a big red X over it. The other was a coffin set on top of a bonfire with a red arrow drawn pointing at it.

Lloyd was cremated two days later with no one to attend a funeral service. His ashes were dumped unceremoniously in a cemetery on the edge of town.

Horror Challenge Topic Suggested by:
Catherine Barson – Kazoo Factory

MUSIC TO THE EARS

Yang was a young boy when his parents dropped him off at the entrance to the Shanxi Province toy factory compound. At the age of twelve, a full understanding of the life that was ahead of him was elusive at best. His parents had simply explained to him that they could no longer feed him. It was time for him to be conscripted to the factory.

It made no difference to Yang. Since his family could not afford the tuition for the only school in his town, he received no education. His clothes were old and ragged, and the children who lived nearby teased him and called him "the rag boy." There would be no friends to miss from his former life. Truly, his prospects at the factory were better than he could have outside of it.

So, with the enthusiasm of a fool who knew no better, he settled into his new life and job in the kazoo factory. At first he thought, What a silly thing this kazoo. It makes no sound of it's own unless one makes a sound into it. Since most were made for customers in the United States, his opinion of Americans was that they must be a foolish lot with no appreciation for real music like his grandfather used to play.

Grandfather had been a popular musician in the Province for most of his life. This high standing in the community gave him access to the wealthy Party members, and his wonderful music made even the most powerful sigh as they listened. In the end, his popularity made him careless. He began discussing his opinions of the government among the local people, and he organized a group that would meet to speak of resistance and rebellion.

When the resistance group was infiltrated by the secret police, Yang's grandfather was brought up on charges and sentenced to life in prison. He had survived three years before word reached the family that he had died from a powerful strain of influenza, though rumor had it he had been killed by the guards for his outspoken ways.

So Yang learned to do what he was told, no matter how difficult or dangerous the task. He began his first week on the metal cutting line. He was good at his job and unafraid of the sharp metal that flew through the machines as it was cut into the various sizes needed to construct a kazoo. His dedication and fearlessness earned him a role as team leader.

In the following eight years, his loyalty and dedication to the company had moved him into one of the most enviable positions in the factory, First Quality Control Inspector. This comfortable job required him to test random kazoos by blowing into them while humming a tune. To make the job more interesting, he had composed several pieces of music. He would even entertain his coworkers on breaks and after work with impromptu concerts of his songs.

Though others often perceived him to be happy with his life, Yang secretly wondered what the world had become outside the walls of the factory compound. For years he had maintained his happy façade with his bosses as he masked his true resentment for his twenty-year agreement with the company. He often dreamed of slipping out under cover of darkness and running far from this place. Unfortunately, he would come back to reality and recognize the futility of such a plan. Instead, his thoughts would turn to suicide as his only way out.

One day, as he was testing products, his eye caught a glimpse of a strangely colored kazoo as it sped past him on the conveyor. Curious, he snatched it up before it could get to the hopper that funneled the finished product to the packaging line. He stood there turning the beautiful instrument in his hands, admiring its brilliant colors and the obvious craftsmanship that made it far better than any other kazoo in the factory. If it sounded as good as it looked, he would keep this one for his performances. He put the metal object to his lips, took a deep breath, and began to hum one of his songs into it. It sounded amazing!

As he took his second deep breath, the kazoo twisted out of his fingers shot into his mouth and down his throat. Only once did he cough as the thing lodged in his larynx. He knew it was there, but he couldn't feel it anymore. Yang grabbed at his neck and bent over until he was upside down, pounding himself on the back. The kazoo would not come out. He reached for his container of water and took a long drink, but still he felt nothing blocking the flow as he swallowed.

Even though he felt fine, he thought he should see the company doctor. Realizing he might be punished for leaving the line, he decided to wait until his shift was over. He kept to himself and did not speak to anyone. There was no discomfort at all, and by the end of the day he forgot all about the beautiful kazoo. Perhaps he had dreamed it.

Washing up after his shift, he decided to go to the meal hall and get something to eat. While waiting in line, he saw his friend, Lin, who greeted him in the usual fashion, "Yang, my friend. I trust you had a productive day? When will you be having your next performance? I met a girl from the Christmas light assembly plant, and she said she would love to hear you. I am very excited to spend a few hours with her."

Yang opened his mouth to speak, and then hesitated, remembering the kazoo. He wondered if it would affect his speech but decided to go on. "Lin, my friend. Is there any point to meeting a girl just to have it determined by the party that you are not to be together?" He covered his mouth, his eyes widening in distress at what he had said.

He opened his mouth to apologize to his friend, but what came out plunged him deeper into his predicament instead. "You must surely realize that we are being forced by our glorious leaders to work in this shit-hole like dogs, and that we have almost no chance of ever leaving!"

Yang tried to stop speaking but the words just kept coming. "You know of old man Lee, right? He started working at this complex when he was fifteen, on contract the same as us. Now he is almost sixty and still working with the plastic toys where he started all those years ago." He clapped his hands over his mouth in shock.

The look on Lin's face spoke volumes. It was as though his fears had been confirmed in the short span of the last few moments. Now he knew for sure that there was no future for him and the girl. "I was foolish to think I could have her. I am sure if the Party meant for us to be together it would have been arranged already." His expression became more somber as he added, "I am sorry, Yang. I don't feel like talking anymore just now."

Lin hurried out of the room, while Yang stood there petrified. What was happening to him? What other hidden thoughts might be revealed if he spoke again? He decided he would not talk to anyone else that night.

After finishing his meal he retired to his sleeping area and quickly fell asleep as always. The next day he was called to the central office early in the morning. As he entered the room, he noticed the concerned look on the face of his boss.

"Yang, welcome. Please have a seat. We are waiting for a
Party official."

Yang did as he was told and sat in one of the chairs in
front of the man's desk. After a few minutes, a heavy set
man in a dark suit was introduced. "Mr. Chin has arrived,
sir." The boss waved his assistant out of the room, and Mr.
Chin to his chair. Taking his seat, the Party official began to
speak.

"Mr. Yang, it has come to the attention of the Party that
you believe somehow that you are being held here against
your will." He straightened his tie, "Let me assure you that
you are here under contract, the one that you signed when
you came to work here. Believe me when I tell you that,
should you insist on saying otherwise to your co-workers, it
might be considered slanderous at best and, shall I say,
dangerous at worst." He eyed Yang waiting for his reply.

"Have you nothing to say?" he demanded. "Surely you
wish to deny these accusations. You have had a very good
record here until now." Yang was nodding as the man
continued to glare.

Mr. Chin asked again, "Your response?"

Yang opened his mouth to speak and the words began to
flow. He began with, "Mr. Chin, you wish me to believe that
you have any of our interests at heart, yet you come here to
threaten me. With what? Imprisonment like my grandfather
suffered at the hands of your glorious party leaders, or would
you just execute me like a dog in an alley. Admit, sir, that this
method appeals most to you and your Party scum." The
more he said, the more he knew his fate was sealed.

The Party official's face was growing redder by the
second. He tried to interrupt the younger man, but Yang
kept on ranting despite his growing panic. "I would rather
cut off the heads of your Party's leaders and piss into their

bleeding necks than hear another word from your bloated pig face."

Finally, he was able to stop. What the hell had he just said? Cut off their heads and piss in their necks? Where in the world had that come from? Wherever, whatever, it didn't matter any more.

Yang didn't see the stun gun pulled from a hidden pocket in Mr. Chin's jacket. When it was pressed against his neck and activated, Yang fell to the floor seeing stars and jerking uncontrollably. The outraged official kicked him in the head and the lights went out.

When Yang regained consciousness, he was in a small cell wearing a uniform. There was a barcode on the loosely fitting shirt. From outside his cell, he could hear someone talking. He called out and asked. "Hey you! Where am I? What is this jail?"

The guard sauntered over and stood on the other side of the bars. He laughed, "You are not in jail, Prisoner Yang. You have been unconscious for nearly two weeks while your trial was held and you were moved here."

"Trial!" Yang asked surprised. "For what?"

"You have been convicted of crimes against the state, Yang. You were sentenced to life in prison here, just like your grandfather before you." There was no opportunity to ask any more questions as the guard walked away laughing.

Yang felt dizzy and sat back down on the steel bed. Suddenly, he was overcome by a fit of violent coughing. Without warning, the colorful kazoo flew out of his mouth and landed in one of his hands. He sat there dumbfounded. He turned it over until he saw the inscription in tiny letters. "Here in this factory our voices are silenced forever. In your country, remember this and never allow your freedom to speak your mind, to remain lodged in your throat."

Next to those tiny words was the usual stamp placed on everything that came out of the factory. 'Made In China'.

Horror Challenge Topic Suggested by:
Heather Badgwell – Drag

OUT FOR DINNER

Marilyn had his body all rolled up nicely in the Persian rug, now all she had to do was get it to the van. He was dead for sure. She had felt for a pulse and even put a small mirror in front of his nose to see if he was breathing. She was positive he was gone.

She needed to pull the van up to the back door. Then, she could drag the rug down the stairs through the kitchen and get him into the trunk without anyone seeing. It would be difficult, but she knew she could pull this off in the end.

Down the stairs and out the back door, she went to get her van. She got in and pulled around to the back yard. Carefully, she backed up to the door and turned off the engine. After she opened the two rear doors, she headed back into the house and up to the bedroom.

Everything was just as she had left it. Not that she had expected to find it any other way. Looking at the large roll of carpet on the floor, she knew there was no way she could carry a full-grown man of his size. She was going to have to drag him. She bent over and grabbed the end of the rug and pulled. "Damn, you are one heavy cowboy!" she complained as she pulled him to the top of the stairs.

Marilyn was thankful for the oak floors. If this house had wall-to-wall carpet, she may not have been able to move the body so easily. As she took two steps down the stairs, she pulled the rug to the halfway point where it teetered on the top step. Taking two more steps, she pulled the rug just enough to upset the equilibrium and allow it to tilt downward. That was when she lost her balance.

The full weight of the man in the rug came sliding down at her, knocking her off her feet. The roll down the steps was painful for her to say the least, and the weight of the rug pushed her all the way to the bottom and then over her as it slid to a stop.

"Shit!" She struggled to get out from under the rug and back on her feet. When she was finally able to stand, she took a moment to straighten her clothes and the blond wig that had been knocked out of place. Determined, she picked up the end of the rug again and continued to drag it through the kitchen and out the back door.

Marilyn breathed a sigh of relief as she let the body flop to the ground next to the van. She was sore from falling down the stairs and winded from exerting herself, so she sat in the back of the van and propped up her feet on the carpet roll to take a break. Pulling a pack of cigarettes from the back pocket of her jeans, she drew one from the pack with her teeth and fired it up. She closed her eyes for a moment and took a nice long drag. It surprised her how good it tasted. Even better than the smoke she often enjoyed after a great romp in the sack.

When she had smoked it down to the filter, she stubbed it out on the ground and put the butt in her pocket. Kneeling down next to the rug, Marilyn grabbed one end and, with a groan, hefted it up over the bumper to let it rest partway into the van. She stepped up, grabbed it again and slid it along the floor until it was all the way in. Now all she had to do was shut the doors and drive away. Should be easy enough.

With her cargo all tucked in, she turned the van around in the driveway and pulled out into the street. No cars were coming and no one was out on the sidewalk. Her getaway would be clean and unnoticed. She followed the street to the freeway ramp, and merged onto the highway traveling southbound.

Dialing through the radio stations, she chose some 80's music but kept the volume low. She didn't want to get too distracted. Traffic was light, but she really didn't like driving at night since the glare of oncoming headlights made it hard to see the road in front of her.

She had traveled about ten miles when she began to hear the moaning coming from the rolled up rug in the back. "Damn!" she said aloud but kept on driving. She assumed the rug was wrapped tight enough to hold the guy until she could pull over at a rest stop. But she was wrong. Before she knew it, the guy was out of the rug crawling toward the front of the van, then he had hold of the steering wheel.

The van was swerving on the highway, crossing between the two lanes as she struggled to regain control of the wheel. The tires screeched as they dug into the pavement and the van rocked back and forth threatening to roll over. With all her might, Marilyn began kicking the guy in the face with the heel of one of her fancy cowboy boots. The man was hanging on for his life and twisted the wheel in the other direction.

Shooting out into the grass of the median between the four lanes of the highway, the van was flying along at over 70 mph. The rough terrain made it almost impossible for her to get control as she reached into the side compartment on the door and grabbed a length of steel pipe that she kept there. Blood spurted everywhere as she bashed the man's face, and he grabbed his nose and howled.

She locked up the brakes long enough to propel him forward driving his head into the console. It was enough to stun him for a moment. Cutting back across the two lanes, the van slid to a halt in the emergency lane at the side of the road.

With the pipe in her hand, she moved to where the man had collapsed on the floor and hit him repeatedly about the head. Shouting one word with each swing of the pipe, she said something like, "Why. Did. You. Have. To. Do. That?" With the last swing, she was pretty sure he wasn't getting back up.

Blood was everywhere and it was evident that she had cracked his skull from the odd shape it had taken. Marilyn grabbed a rag off the floor, wiped the pipe, and returned it to its storage area. She wiped her hands and sat back in the driver's seat. "Geez! What a shitty first date this has turned into," she yelled into the back. Laughing wildly, she threw the van in gear and eased back onto the highway.

About fifteen minutes later, she exited the highway and followed a country road to a small house situated back from the street. She stopped in the driveway and put the van into park, jumped out and walked over to the mailbox to get the mail. There were a few letters and a package addressed to her. As she got back in the van, her heart began to flutter as she saw the return address on the package.

The vampire romance novel she had won in an online giveaway had finally arrived! She had been waiting weeks for that book! "Woo-hoo!" she yelled as she popped the van in gear and continued up the long gravel drive to park behind the house. Throwing open the van door, she hopped up and walked into the house with the mail in her hand and a smile on her face.

As she entered the kitchen, her smile faded. The basket of laundry was exactly where she had left it before she went out earlier.

"Daddy!" she yelled toward the other room as she tossed her mail on the table.

An older man shuffled out of the living room.

"What's all the commotion?" he answered rubbing the stubble on his chin.

"I asked you to do the laundry while I was out getting dinner." She looked at him with her hands on her hips.

"Sorry I forgot." Ashamed, he looked at the floor.

"Well, you're lucky you are good with the fillet knife or I'd have to beat your ass for that." She softened her tone and added as she washed her hands in the sink, "Now go on out to the van and bring in the meat. It made a real mess on the way home."

"Sorry," he said again as he shuffled out through the door.

As he was unloading the van, Marilyn sat down at the table and opened the package she had gotten in the mail. Smiling again, she cracked open her new autographed book

Horror Challenge Topic Suggested by:
Lynn Worton – A Bar of Soap

TINY MONSTERS

"Cleanliness is next to Godliness" is what Lynda's grandmother would always say to her when she protested bath time as a little girl. Lynda never truly understood the meaning of that saying until she had a child of her own. Taking Granny's words to heart, she figured her six-year old son, Tommy, must be possessed by the Devil.

Bath time was always a struggle with Tommy. He had more excuses not to wash himself than most kids his age could ever come up with. When her favorite shop had a basket full of clear soaps with tiny little monsters in the middle, she hoped she had found something that could motivate him to get into the tub without an argument.

"These soaps are really interesting," she said to the shop owner. "Where do they come from?"

"Well, obviously someone ordered them, but I'm not sure who to ask," the woman replied looking in the basket. "They sure are popular though. The basket was full when we opened this morning."

"I can see why. My son will love this!" She was excited as she dug through the soaps that were left in the bowl. "The label says that when water comes in contact with the creatures, they expand to their actual size."

"Yes, I've seen things like that before. It's been around for years. Usually the things are dinosaurs or animal sponges, but these are really unique, and so detailed." The woman held a bar in her hand and examined it. "They swell up to about ten times their original size when they soak in water from what I remember of them."

Lynda finally settled on one bar that had three prehistoric looking fish and another with something that looked like a cross between a bear and a dog. "I'll take these two." She set them on the counter and dug for her wallet.

That night, she had a surprise for Tommy at bath time. "Tommy!" she called. "It's time to take a bath."

"Awww, Mom! I was playing with Sparky. He was doing some tricks. Can't I get a bath tomorrow?"

"Well, if you don't get a bath tonight, you won't get to try out this new kind of soap I bought today. Here look at this." She handed the two bars of soap to him.

He looked at the soaps with wide eyes. "These are so cool, Mom. Yeah… I guess me and Sparky can play later." He was climbing the stairs as his faithful dog followed.

Lynda was smiling when she heard the bath water running a few minutes later. Finally she had found something that would get him to pay more attention to his hygiene, even if it involved a bribe.

For the next several nights, she didn't even have to ask Tommy to get his bath. Instead, the problem she had was getting him out of the tub. After ten days, he was happy to report that he was almost down to the fish and he could start on the other one in a couple of days.

Lynda returned to the shop the next day to get some more of that soap, but unfortunately she was informed that it had sold out the day she bought it. She decided that she would just have to enjoy it while it lasted and think of something else when it was gone.

That night, Tommy ate his dinner faster than usual. When he was finished, he headed up the stairs to the bathroom and started the bath water running. Sparky followed him into the bathroom and took his place on the bath mat in front of the shower. Tommy got undressed and stepped into the tub. He made the water as hot as he could stand because it helped the soap to melt away faster. He eased himself into the water. When he was settled, he grabbed his bar of soap and threw it into the water between his legs.

This was the night, he thought, as he watched the water come in contact with the fish. Just as he expected, they began to swell and grow. And they grew and grew. At first, he was excited by how big they were getting but when he thought he saw one of them move, he called out, "Mom?"

Downstairs, Lynda was loading the dishwasher. She thought she heard a noise coming from the bathroom, but went back to work thinking how excited Tommy must be to finally get his prize.

Then she heard the screaming. Something was wrong! She ran from the kitchen and bounded up the stairs taking them two at a time. The screaming had become shrill and Sparky was barking and growling as she turned the doorknob and threw the door open.

It was beyond any nightmare she could have ever imagined. Sparky was drenched in blood and trying to pull something out of the tub. She couldn't see Tommy at all, just three giant fish thrashing in the tub. Sparky had hold of one of them by the tail as it thrashed and snapped it's huge jaws at him.

Her scream was shrill enough to get the attention of the fish for a second before they turned back to their feast. Fighting the instinct to pass out, Lynda looked for something to use to get the fish out of the tub. She grabbed the black rubber plunger that sat next to the toilet and began beating the fish with it until one of them turned and bit off the rubber head and swallowed it. Sparky lost his grip on the tail and was trying to get into the tub to get at the monsters.

Without the plunger head, she was left with a sharp wooden handle. In a rage, she began stabbing the fish over and over until the feeding frenzy was replaced by the final desperate flips of fins and tails. She dropped the handle and threw the dying fish on the floor desperately looking for Tommy in the bloody water. All she found was a badly chewed arm, and she fell to the floor overcome.

Lynda suddenly sat up screaming in the bed. She felt the sweat dripping from her brow as she glanced around the room and listened for any unusual sound. She jumped out of bed and ran to the bathroom. When she turned on the light, everything looked normal. There were two bars of soap in the soap dish on the edge of the tub and no signs of blood anywhere. She noticed that the soap Tommy had been using this week was almost melted down to the colorful fish.

Her heart pounded in her chest as she threw the bar with the fish into the toilet and flushed it. She watched as it swirled in the bowl and then disappeared. Determined, she flushed it three more times just to be sure it was gone. The remaining bar was too large to flush, so she headed downstairs to the kitchen. Pulling the trash bin from under the sink, she lifted some trash out and buried the soap so it couldn't be seen, then slid the bin back in place and closed the door.

As she washed her hands in the sink, she muttered, "I don't care if that boy ever takes another bath, EVER!" Then she switched off the light and headed back to bed.

Horror Challenge topic suggested by:
Mary Holder — Coat Pocket

DEEP POCKETS

Alonzo had a thing for fine clothing. Even when he was in high school, he always tried to dress like he was stepping out of a men's fashion magazine. It was the reason he got his first job when he was old enough to work… to buy clothes.

While living at home with his parents, he was able to afford the designer labels he craved. After he turned twenty, however, his parents invited him to find other living arrangements. The meager income from his job as a coffee jockey at the local Java House put a cramp in his wardrobe budget. It was a difficult lifestyle change, and he was reduced to shopping at thrift stores to feed his habit.

On this particular day, Alonzo happened by a small rundown consignment shop on the south side of town. As he pored over the racks, he was thrilled to find something he had never seen there before, a jacket by a talented but little known designer, Ricardo Demona. It was a beautifully tailored piece made of a fabric he couldn't quite name. He held it up to admire its shimmer in the light of the shop.

He carried the jacket to the counter and got the attention of the clerk working there. "Hey, excuse me. Would you happen to know what kind of fabric this is? There isn't any label."

"Nah, I never saw anything like it before. Maybe it's some kind of silk blend or something."

Alonzo was getting excited. Here was an obvious, one-of-a-kind designer jacket, and if only it fit... He tried it on and enjoyed his sudden luck. It fit as though it were custom tailored for him. In fact, it fit him better than the only custom tailored suit jacket he owned. Then, a hesitation... In his excitement, he hadn't even checked the price. He was afraid to look now thinking that, since it was so very fine, it was probably out of his price range. When he finally got the nerve to look, he had to force himself not to let out a yell. It was only ten bucks!

He was afraid maybe someone had switched the tags on the jacket, so he hurried to the counter to pay for it. Surely the guy at the counter would know whether or not the tag had been switched. Relieved to find that it was the right price, he quickly paid for it and left the store.

Whistling as he walked down the street carrying his treasure in a plastic garment bag, Alonzo went straight home so he could try to match it up with some trousers from his now shrinking wardrobe. As he entered his apartment, he locked the door behind him. Leaning back against the door, he hugged the bag to his chest and savored the moment before hurrying to his single bedroom where he hung the bag on the back of the door to remove the plastic.

In the light of his room, the jacket looked even better than in the store. He dug through the rack in his closet, holding up every pair of pants he had next to the jacket. At first he thought it was strange that every pair of pants seemed to match it perfectly. Then he did the unthinkable. He opened the bottom drawer of his dresser and dug out the only pair of jeans he owned.

"Damn!" he said, holding the jeans up to the jacket. "It's true. This jacket goes with everything!" He hastily stepped out of the slacks he was wearing and slipped on the designer jeans. Putting the jacket on, he stepped up to the full-length mirror. Tears came to his eyes. It was the most amazing outfit he had ever worn, and he was wearing jeans!

He decided to go for a walk and maybe squeeze some comments from his friends down the street. He took his wallet from his other jacket and got his keys. Inserting the wallet into the breast pocket of the new jacket, he had a strange sensation. The wallet didn't seem to reach the bottom of the pocket.

"Weird." Alonzo patted the jacket feeling for the wallet, but there was nothing. He felt around the bottom of the jacket, thinking maybe the pocket was torn and had allowed it to fall to the seam. Again there was nothing. Truly puzzled now, he pulled the jacket open and stuck his hand into the pocket. Sure enough there was no lining in the pocket and his hand went down into the jacket.

Perhaps he might find the wallet if he kept feeling around, but even when he took the jacket off and shoved his entire arm into the pocket, he couldn't feel the bottom of the jacket, or even the sides of the fabric inside. Now he was really at a loss as to what was going on.

He carried the jacket into the kitchen and opened the pantry door to get his broom. Holding the broom by the brush, he shoved the broom handle into the pocket as far as it could go. From the outside, there was no sign that the broom handle was inside the jacket. Even when he turned the brush head and made it swing back and forth, there was nothing impeding the handle.

Easily twice the length of the jacket, the handle of the broom had to be pushing against the bottom seam of the lining, but Alonzo couldn't feel a thing. As he moved it around some more, he lost his grip and the entire head of the broom disappeared into the pocket and was gone. This scared the hell out of him and he dropped the jacket. It crumpled to the floor. Fastidious to a fault, he couldn't bear to leave it there. He quickly picked it up and hung it over the back of the chair.

Some time went by before he felt around the outside of the jacket trying to find evidence of the broom handle, but he couldn't feel it anywhere. Maybe if he dropped something in the pocket that would make a noise, he could find where in the jacket it might be.

Alonzo looked around the kitchen for something to use, and spotted his iPod. "Cool. I can use the small plug-in speakers so I will hear the music no matter where it ends up," he thought as he dug through the drawer until he found the speakers. He turned on the iPod and checked the battery. It was fully charged, so he plugged in the speakers, scrolled to a playlist, and pushed play. Turning the volume up to the max, he walked over to the jacket still hanging on the chair, pulled the lapel back and dropped it into the pocket.

He got down on his knees next to the amazing article of clothing and listened as the iPod fell deeper and deeper into the pocket until he could no longer hear it. "What the hell?" He really wanted to know where this stuff was going. How was he going to find out? His eyes fell on the knife set on the counter. Maybe he could just cut the opening of the pocket wide enough to fit his head through the hole, and then he could use a flashlight and look for himself.

He had seen the flashlight in the drawer where he had found the speakers. He stood up and got it out, checking to make sure it was working. Taking a knife from the block on the counter, he set the flashlight on the table next to him as he carefully cut the pocket on both sides. Exchanging the knife for the flashlight, he turned it on again and thrust it into the pocket. It felt like a cavern with no walls in there.

He picked up the jacket and turned it upside down pushing his head into the enlarged hole of a pocket.

Alonzo didn't realize that by turning the jacket upside down, he was allowing whatever was at the bottom of the pit to fall toward him, along with his wallet and the broom. Even though he was holding the flashlight, he didn't see what was coming for him.

If someone had been standing in the kitchen that day, they would have seen a ridiculous looking man with a jacket over his head one moment, and the next moment watched as an empty jacket fell to the floor. The screams that faded away to silence inside the lining may have revealed his fate, but with no one there to witness, did it even happen?

When Alonzo had been missing for several weeks, his parents gave up hope of ever finding him. His landlord demanded that they clean out his apartment, so they put all of his things into boxes, loaded them onto a truck, and dropped them at the nearest thrift store. Everything was donated except the jacket. His father had thought it was unlike anything he had ever seen and it fit him so perfectly! He hung it on a hanger in the back of his car and drove home with it shimmering in the sunlight. He figured if he would have the occasion to wear it, he might be able to somehow feel close to his son once again.

Horror Challenge Topic suggested by:
Lisa Cagle – Computer Mouse
Jennifer Bonges – Group
Mallory Anne-Marie Forbes – Pummeled

THE HOUSE GUEST

It was 3:00 a.m. and Dan's computer was back on again. He knew this only because he had been lying in bed debating whether or not to get up and empty his bloated bladder. He finally succumbed to the call. As he walked past his office, he noticed the glow of the monitor.

He was sure he had put it into sleep mode after he had finished up earlier, but there it was on again. He trekked into the bathroom and took care of business, but before he could go back to bed he was going to turn off that damn computer. After all, what's the point of having an energy saving feature that doesn't save energy?

He went into the office and sat down at his desk. On the monitor was a Wikipedia page, a page that he had never seen before. More disturbing than that, it was a page he would never have visited at all, "Heaven's Gate". For some reason the name sounded familiar to him, so out of curiosity, he started to read. Now he remembered why it had sounded familiar. In March of 1997, thirty-nine members of a religious cult had committed suicide believing that a comet passing near the earth would be their vehicle to a more perfect world.

As he read, Dan wondered why this page should be on his computer. What was the significance? Better yet, how did it get there? He had moved into this San Diego neighborhood only five years ago. It really creeped him out when he realized that this very neighborhood was where the tragedy had occurred. He was so engrossed that he didn't notice the mouse moving next to him until he saw the pointer on the screen move to the X in the upper corner of the page and the browser closed.

Dan sat frozen. His heart was pounding in his chest, but he waited to see what would happen next. He watched the cordless laser mouse move around on the pad as if someone was working with it. It clicked on the icon for his chat program and it opened. What now? He moved his hands away from the keyboard. If whatever this was decided to do some typing, he didn't want to be in it's way. Sure enough, the keys started pressing themselves to type.

"Bo, why do you continue to ignore these messages? I need instruction. The others are asking questions. We can't open the door. I fear we are lost."

Dan felt sick to his stomach. If one of the people who had killed themselves that day was trying to send a message, how many of them might be in his house at this moment? The mouse moved, minimized the chat window, and opened the browser again. This time it entered HeavensGate.com into the browser, and the website for the cult opened. After all these years was it still online?

It was a primitive site, but the mouse seemed to know exactly where to click, opening page after page as if it were searching for something. Hesitating on a page, then clicking the back button to click another link, it was obviously looking for something specific. Within fifteen minutes, Dan had seen every page on the site. The bits he had been able to read made him fully aware that these people had some serious mental health issues. Now their spirits seemed to be hanging out in his house, using his computer.

This series of events repeated for the remainder of the hour and each time the question asked in the chat window was the same. At exactly 4:00 a.m. the activity stopped and the computer went back into sleep mode, and Dan got up and went into the living room. By 5:30 a.m., he was still sitting on the sofa thinking about it. He didn't feel scared, but this discovery was upsetting.

He couldn't shake the thought that the crazy ghost members of a death cult group had invaded his beautiful half-million dollar home. There must be some way to get them to leave. He called his employer and requested a sick day, and then spent most of the day researching techniques for ridding a home of malicious spirits. There were hundreds of suggestions, but none of them seemed like an effective solution to his specific problem.

According to all the websites, it was possible that it wasn't his house, but his computer that had become possessed. It appeared it was sometimes possible to communicate with the dead and, through gentle persuasion, guide them to the light that would free them from this earthly plane. It didn't take much for Dan to make a conscious decision. He would try to convince the confused to go to the light.

Exhausted, he went to sleep early that night around 7:00 p.m. He set his alarm for 2:00 a.m. thinking he would wake up, send his message and solve his problem. The alarm went off at 2:00 and he got right up, made some coffee and a bagel, and then headed into the office to wait for his unwelcome guests.

The computer was in sleep mode as usual when 3:00 a.m. rolled around. Right on cue, the mouse began to move and the screen blinked to life. All programs were closed until the Internet browser opened. Dan watched as the search engine Dogpile.com came into view. He had no idea that search engine still existed, but the search terms were entered for Heaven's Gate. The mouse moved to Wikipedia and clicked the link.

Dan was waiting for the chat window. In a few minutes it should open. Sure enough, the cursor moved to close the browser. The chat window opened and the message typed itself on the keyboard. "Bo, why do you continue to ignore these messages? I need instruction. The others are asking questions. We can't open the door. I fear we are lost."

This was his chance. He typed into the keyboard. "Forget the door. Turn and walk into the light. It is your way to the next level." Then he sat back and waited.

After a few minutes a response came.

"Who is this?" it asked.

"Shit!" Dan hadn't expected it to ask any questions, so he typed, "This is Bo. Move away from the door. It won't open for you. Walk into the light."

Again there was a hesitation.

One word was typed in all caps.

"LIAR!"

The screen went dark. Dan could still see everything in the room since he had left the light on in the hall. He was watching to see if the mouse would move again. Without warning, it flew at his face and smacked him right between the eyes with the force of a major league pitch.

The impact hurt so much that his eyes began to water profusely. He tried to regain a bit of composure when suddenly all hell broke loose. The books on the bookshelf began flying at him along with every bit of bric-a-brac he had collected over the years. A Star Wars action figure struck him in the ear and he had to pull the pose-able arm out of his ear canal to get it off. When the shelves were emptied, his collection of favorite things rose up from the floor and pummeled him again. The empty shelves shook until they tore themselves apart. That's when he made a break for the door, which slammed in his face and locked.

The only light in the room now was the glow from the streetlights outside. A veritable tornado of broken wood, collector's toys and books threatened to continue beating him to death. They threw everything at him... except the computer! Those people were all computer geeks in life. Why not in death?

Dan dove for the desk, grabbed the monitor, and climbed under it. Then with his back to the wall, he held the monitor at the opening of the desk like a warrior holding a shield. For the rest of the hour he crouched under the desk wondering when it would end.

At exactly 4:00 a.m., everything simply dropped to the floor and all was quiet. He waited for a few minutes to make sure it was safe before crawling out from under the desk. The room was destroyed. Every single item in the room was torn to pieces, except the desk, the keyboard, and the case containing the computer processor. Pens, pencils and large splinters of wood stuck out from the walls like porcupine quills. Every book, page, and paper was ripped to shreds.

Stunned, Dan walked cautiously to the door, turned the knob and was extremely relieved when it opened. He turned back to the desk and unplugged all the cables from the computer. He stacked the monitor and keyboard on top of the case and carried it to the trashcan in the garage. The he opened the garage door and rolled the trashcan to the curb.

When he went back into the house, he returned to his office. He turned the lock knob on the inside of the door and closed the door from the hallway. Grabbing a beer from the kitchen, Dan twisted the cap as he headed for the couch. He commented aloud that, "no matter what, I will never have another computer, at least as long as I am living in this house."

From the office there came a whisper of a voice, "Yes, as long as you are living."

Footnote: In 1997, 39 members of the Heaven's Gate cult committed mass suicide in an upscale subdivision in San Diego California. They believed that they would ascend to a UFO in the tail of the Hale Bopp comet. Their website remains online to this day.

Horror Challenge Topic suggested by:
Peggy Sue Lea Martinez – Midwife

The Special Delivery

Madelyn was a nurse at a big city hospital when she made the decision to quit her job and become a midwife in rural America. After careful consideration, she decided to move to the mountains in Tennessee.

When she had settled into her tiny house, she wasted no time contacting the local social worker's office. She hoped to work with the women in mountain country who lived too far from hospitals and could not afford the transportation to travel into the city to receive care from traditional doctors. Needless to say, she was delighted to receive her first assignment with a woman known only as Carolee.

Carolee lived in a rustic log home on the side of a mountain that had no electricity or running water. When Madelyn first met her, she was already six months into her pregnancy. During their first appointment, Madelyn discussed nutrition and helped the mother-to-be develop a plan for when it was time to deliver the baby. Since she would need a way to contact Madelyn, she had been provided a simple cell phone with a solar charger and taught how to dial her number.

Madelyn was concerned that her four-wheel drive SUV was not able to negotiate the road all the way to the cabin. She had to hike the last mile on every visit through the rough terrain. Potentially, this could be a problem on the day Carolee went into labor. She had tried many times to convince her to move to the local women's shelter at least until after the baby was delivered, but Carolee would have nothing to do with it.

After two months of weekly visits, the call came in the middle of the night. "Yes? Is this Carolee?" The woman on the other end sounded as if she were in pain. "I'll grab my things and come right away!" She disconnected the call and grabbed the bag she had prepared for such occasions. After nearly an hour of driving, she was finally walking the distance to the tiny home on the hill. As she drew closer, she could see light coming from the windows. She smiled to herself as she thought how cozy this cabin in the woods looked at night.

Suddenly, a loud howl broke through the serenity. Fearing it could be a wolf, Madelyn picked up her already fast pace and was relieved when she reached the door. When she knocked, a muffled voice instructed her to enter. Carolee was lying on the makeshift sofa holding her stomach.

"We need to get you into the bedroom," Madelyn said as she put her arm around the woman and helped her walk to the bed. "I'm going to get some water so we can clean up when we're done." She made sure Carolee was as comfortable as possible before heading to the pump in the kitchen. She grabbed a large pan sitting next to the wood stove and pumped enough water to fill it.

Carrying it back to the bedroom, she found Carolee lying on her back. Her cotton dress was wet with amniotic fluid, and she was moaning. Madelyn pulled a rustic wooden chair to the edge of the bed and leaned in to inspect the situation. She was holding a flashlight because the light from the burning candles was too dim to see clearly. As she shone it toward the woman's birth canal, she wasn't quite sure what she was seeing.

"Honey, are you feeling all right? Something doesn't seem right here." She inched the chair a little closer.

Carolee answered with a loud moan as she pushed. Madelyn reached out to help the baby and found it necessary to put down the flashlight. She saw something moving now and she grabbed it, gently pulling the newborn to help it make its way into the world. In a moment, the baby was free and in her hands, but it didn't feel like any baby she had handled before. She placed the infant on Carolee's stomach and the woman was happy to cradle it in her arms.

Madelyn was desperate to see how the baby actually looked. She feared that it might be grossly deformed from the way that it felt. She picked up the flashlight again and shone it on the baby. She screamed, letting the flashlight fall from her slippery hands. The baby lying on its mother's stomach looked like a writhing pile of flesh. She couldn't make out any human features at all.

"Oh God, Carolee! I'm so sorry! I just don't know what to do!"

"Oh, don't worry." The new mother said calmly. "He's just trying to make up his mind what to become." She was smiling as she watched her child moving on her stomach.

"I'm sorry. I don't understand..." Madelyn replied in a state of shock.

"I knew you didn't know about me, and that was why I agreed to use you for this night." As she spoke, she laid the baby on the bed beside her and began to rise.

"What are you talking about?" Madelyn started backing toward the bedroom door.

"I didn't need you to help me deliver my baby..." Her voice faltered and lowered as she spoke. She seemed to be growing larger, and her face was changing.

Madelyn turned to run and was tripped by a clawed hand grabbing her ankle. She turned to see what only seconds ago had been Carolee, had now transformed into some kind of a large beast. "I could have delivered the baby myself. What I needed was some help feeding him."

"What the hell are you?" screamed Madelyn.

The voice coming from "Carolee" was low and heavy now. "I knew when I met you that you'd never seen a shape shifter before, and that made you perfect for this, this job." It was smiling at her with a mouthful of large jagged teeth. "Like I said, I needed help feeding him." With that, one clawed hand pinned Madelyn to the floor while the other dug its claws into her thigh. It squeezed with a vice grip that shattered her bone. With a quick yank, it tore her leg from her body.

The pain was so intense her mind began to reel and the room spun as her leg was carried to the bed. "Carolee" tore off a piece of flesh with her teeth. Madelyn was fading quickly, but she watched in horror as the meat was offered to the baby, which had now assumed the appearance of a smaller version of its mother.

As Madelyn bled out on the floor, the creature sat down on the bed and cradled her baby in her arms. "I think I'll call you Carl, you handsome little devil." She bit off another chunk of leg meat and gave it to the baby as it gobbled it up and growled with delight.

Horror Challenge Topics suggested by:
Angie Edwards – Attic
Zack Parris – Defenestrate
Tanya Contois – Porcelain Dolls, Clowns and Jesters

THE CLEANING

Rob kissed Becky on the forehead as he was walking out the door. "Bye, honey." As an afterthought, he stopped on the sidewalk. "Are you going to go through the attic today for the yard sale coming up on Saturday?"

"That's the plan as soon as you pull out of the driveway." She motioned for him to get going.

"I can do without anything but the golf clubs…" He looked worried. "…And the comic book collection." He stood there thinking until she crossed her arms and gave him 'the look'. "Okay, Okay, I'm going." He blew her a kiss, "Love you!" and walked toward the car.

"Love you too." She called after him. She stood in the doorway until he had backed the car out of the drive, and then closed the door.

Walking through the kitchen, she stopped to retrieve a cup from the shelf and pour herself a cup of coffee. She stood and drank it straight without cream or sugar and thought about the task before her. There was a lot of stuff in the attic to go through, most of it things collected from her childhood and Rob's. Some were wedding gifts they'd never used. There were several boxes filled with things that had been moved up there during other cleaning sessions and forgotten over time.

She grabbed a hand full of trash bags and a flashlight from the pantry and tucked them under her arm. Climbing the stairs to the second floor, Becky turned down the hall to where the cord hung from the attic door. She set her coffee on the floor and reached up to pull the door down. After unfolding the ladder, she picked up her coffee and carefully climbed the rungs up into the shadowy attic.

The windows on either end of the roof allowed some light to filter into the large room, but she would need the flashlight to go through the many boxes. "Where to start?" she said aloud. "Who wants to get packed for the garage sale first?" Silence was the answer. "I think I'll start with the doll collection," she continued as she turned on the flashlight and beamed it into the corners of the room.

The attic was situated along the peak of the roof, its walls sharply slanted on the sides. Becky had to duck to keep from hitting her head. When she finally found what she was looking for, she was surprised to find the doll boxes scattered on the floor lying open and empty. At first, she had a flash of anger thinking Rob must have gone through them and left it this way. However, she knew that the only time he ever came up here was when she asked him to lift a heavy box for her.

She knelt on the floor to make a cursory inspection of the mess when suddenly the door to the attic slammed shut. Startled, she jumped, hitting her head on the cross beam of the roof. "Shit!" she said, grabbing her head. She felt the spot where it had struck the roof and then looked at her hand to see if there was blood on it. There was a little bit on her fingertips, but nothing to be concerned about.

Becky walked to the door and shone her flashlight on it. The ladder was folded up and the door was definitely shut. "Now how did this happen?" She bent over and tried pushing the door down. There was a rustling behind her, and she whipped around with the flashlight in her hand.

The beam fell across a group of dolls standing a few feet from her. They were figures from her porcelain doll collection, three pale-faced girls in fancy dresses, two clowns, and a jester, all of them standing there. Were they really looking at her? "This isn't real," she said aloud. "You can't stand without your display…" She stopped talking as the dolls began moving toward her. "What's going on? What do you want?" she asked, as one of the clowns stepped out in front of the group.

Becky's mind was racing. She had seen movies about things like this before, but this was real. In the movies, the situation always ended badly. The first thing that came to mind was to grab that damned clown and defenestrate the bastard. If she could get to the window, watching as it was thrown out might make the others think twice about trying something. At the same time, she was terrified at the thought that they might be faster than her and do something to her before she could get the window open.

The group moved in closer with the clown in the lead. Its painted face seemed to mimic her fear, mocking her as it advanced. "Stop right there, or I'll…" What would she do? "I'll rip your heads off!" she yelled.

The clown raised its arm and seemed to point at her, but she still had the trash bags under her arm. Perhaps if it had been able to speak, it may have explained that they were afraid of being taken to the yard sale. As the clown motioned to the trash bags, she thought he was pointing at her. She panicked and took a step back.

The folding ladder beneath Becky caught on her foot as she fell through the opening in the floor. Her chin struck hard against the floor in front of her as she dropped and her neck was jerked back, snapping it. No sound could be heard as she slipped from consciousness and flopped forward hanging by her foot still tangled in the ladder.

The only witnesses to the tragic accident were the wonderful dolls of her treasured collection. These were the dolls to whom she had promised that she would never, ever let anyone take them away from her. She had made the solemn oath when she was only eight years old, 'cross her heart and hope to die'.

VOLUME III

THE HORROR CHALLENGE

Horror Challenge Topic Suggested by:
Mary Holder – Voodoo

SLAY IT FORWARD

James was desperate as the team meeting dragged on and on. His boss, Renee was a total bitch and he was beginning to imagine his third scenario of her violent death when she called out his name.

"James, what is your plan?" He knew she was speaking English but all he heard was screeching sounds as he came out of his daydream.

"Uh… what was that again?" He surely had no idea what she had said.

"Look James, the rest of the team has been working hard on their goals, the least you could do is pay them the respect of listening." Her face was contorting and he swore she looked just like a witch in a movie, a really ugly one.

There was a long pause before he spoke, "I'm uh… sorry I can't stop thinking about my vacation, they were stating their goals for the quarter, right?"

The others looked at him with looks of 'here it comes' as she let go on him, "Perhaps you should extend your vacation indefinitely Mr. Roarke."

He felt the heat in his reddened face as he read from the paper he had prepared for the meeting. The others in the room pretended interest in his goals in the hopes that this meeting would end soon, but their hopes were unfounded. No sooner had James finished reading his goals, Renee launched into another attack that was somehow also directed at the entire team.

"Mr. Roarke has proven that not even one of this team has given us a clue what we will be doing in the coming quarter to increase sales." She motioned for everyone to pass their papers to her, "Everyone hand their papers over. I am so appalled that I will now have to take these home tonight and spend my evening trying to figure out how to get this worked out myself. Thank you all so much for your useless input. We'll go over my changes first thing in the morning."

A wave of temporary relief swept through the room, though everyone knew that tomorrow morning would be hell revisited. A certain amount of envy was directed at James, who by tomorrow morning would be waking up in a hotel overlooking the beaches at Gulf Shores.

As they walked back to their cubicles, Hank caught up to James, "Dude, you are lucky, you won't have to be at that meeting tomorrow. Wanna trade bodies? I'll go on your southern tour and you can have my life and my wife for a week."

Now this said a lot about the feelings of the others on his team. Hank's wife was quite an attractive woman and for him to offer her up that casually said a lot about how much he hated this job. Tempting as the proposition was, James knew better than to even pretend to accept it. It would only cause a lot of problems later and he really did need the time off.

So he simply responded, "Right now I would kill to be free of that bitch Renee, and I'd probably be the most popular guy in the company if I did."

"That's true, so go ahead and enjoy the vacation, don't worry about us, we might survive." Hank slapped him on the back and went to his own cube.

After work he headed straight for the beach, so when the sun came up the next morning, he was sitting on his small balcony overlooking the peaceful ocean while he waited for his coffee to finish brewing. He had retrieved his tablet computer before he sat down and was reviewing his route and plan. It included two days here, two in Biloxi Miss. for gambling, and then his final destination of New Orleans. On the last stop he intended to party like there was no tomorrow before heading home. For all he knew he wouldn't have a job when he returned, so he was going to really live it up.

While he reviewed his itinerary and message popped up on the screen. It was from one of his co-workers. The message stated that earlier in the morning his boss was looking for him, apparently unaware that he was on vacation. She wanted some reports he had given her the previous week and was upset that she did not have them.

James simply responded, "Tell her to look in the stack of papers on her desk. By now the reports should be about four inches from the top." Then he signed it, "See you in Hell."

After that, James attitude was ruined for the day. There was nothing left to do but crack open a bottle of bourbon. It was the good stuff and he certainly had too much before lunch. He passed out about two in the afternoon and was out until ten that evening. In all it was a wasted day and he vowed that from then until the end of his vacation, he was not going to look at any screen that could show a message.

After watching two movies on the hotel cable, he went to sleep. Tomorrow he was supposed to be headed for Biloxi. He expected when he got there was when the partying would get started. He was wrong.

Biloxi wasn't what it used to be. After the hurricanes of the last couple of years, the only places that were decent enough to go to were all located along Beach Boulevard. All of the new construction had a lot of the roads torn up and made the traffic back up for miles. Once he checked into his hotel, the only places he wanted to go were within walking distance.

Two days of gambling did not pan out either. He lost five hundred on the blackjack table, two on the slots, and another three hundred and change at the craps table. On the eve of his drive to New Orleans, he was laying on his bed in his hotel room hoping to salvage his vacation over the next two days.

"It has to be better there. It just has to. I need something to take my mind off the job just for a day." He was talking to himself again. He hated when he did that.

The following day found him in the French Quarter in New Orleans. His hotel room was beautiful. Even after all of the flooding he had heard about, this town was rocking. He spent that first night drifting from club to club, taking in the flavor of creole music and even dancing with some women who had approached him at his table. Things were indeed turning around.

After many drinks and the women had gone back to their hotel with some other guys in tow, he found himself wandering the streets. As he walked along, he reached into his pocket to check his phone for the time and slipping from his fingers, it fell on the sidewalk. As he stood from picking it up he saw a sign on a shop that caught his attention. It simply read "House of Voodoo" in white letters against a black background.

When you are as buzzed as James was at that given moment, you are bound to try just about anything once, and as he shoved the phone back into his pocket, he stumble toward the door. Once inside, the sounds from the street seemed to be sealed outside and the only sounds breaking the hush of the shop came from a young couple looking at a display of Magical oils and Charm Bags. As he turned around, he was standing directly in front of a wall of Voodoo dolls.

He picked up a doll and looked at it, smiling. He thought about his boss and her torture of him and his coworkers and longed to give her some torture of her own. If only these dolls were real, he'd…

"Hello mon, da magic you seek isn't here."

The man's voice from behind him made his heart skip a beat as he jumped from the sound of it. "Uh, where did you come from?"

"I been watchin you, mon. There be a dark hole in your spirit that needs to be sated." He brushed a few of his long dreadlocks back from his face. "Da magic you seek isn't here. The real magic is up dem stairs." He pointed at a thick beaded curtain that concealed any sign of a stairway. "Go ahead mon, take a look. I be right dere to help wit what you seek." He motioned with both hands as if pushing James along.

James was hesitant, this was just too strange especially right now in his condition. "I, would but I have to…"

"What you gon do? Call dat boss Renee and ask her permission mon? if you want I call her for you!" He challenged James in a way that he couldn't refuse, so he went. As he passed through the heavy beads, a cold rush of air greeted him and it had a somewhat sobering effect. It made plodding up the rickety wooden steps less difficult and obviously safer since many of the boards were warped out of shape. Carefully he reached the second floor. To his surprise, the Rastaman was already there. He was sitting on the sofa taking a long draw off a hookah.

As he blew out a cloud of green smoke, he coughed, "What took you so long mon? Have a seat and let's talk bout that boss lady, you be needin revenge now." He offered the pipe hose to James.

"No thanks, I don't smoke." He waved the offer away.

"This be strong Mojo, mon. You take the smoke and we make the deal." Again he held out the pipe. "No smoke, no deal."

"Well, alright then." James took the pipe mouthpiece and put it to his lips and took a small drag. The smoke tasted spicy and good. He decided to give it a big hit. As he coughed out his lungs he felt something moving in his hand. When he looked, it was a long slim green snake writhing and ready to strike.

"Aaarrrgghh!" he yelled, dropped the reptile and it returned to its original form. Even though the pipe hose turned snake had startled him, he felt warm and happy. He wanted to know more about getting revenge on his boss. "So what do I have to do? How much is it going to cost me?" he asked pulling out his wallet.

"It be easy James, and for da revenge you want, almost free." He turned and reached to a table behind him. When his hand came back it was holding a very nondescript voodoo doll. In fact the only human features it had were a head, torso, arms and legs. "You take dis image home and keep him in a safe place. When a day does come and you revenge with boss complete, you dismember *him*, and then burn. Simple!" and he grinned showing full his yellow teeth.

He held out the doll to James, but when he tried to take it, the man didn't let go. Instead he moved closer to James and looked into his eyes. "There be one more ting, James. There is no second try, no change of mind. You soon to dismember and burn da image or you pay with you very soul." Then he let go of the doll and sat back cackling with laughter.

James looked at the doll in his hand and when he looked back the man was gone. He sat there for a moment, stunned. "What just happened?" he asked himself as he looked at the doll again. It seemed harmless enough, but the things the Rastaman had said filled him with dread. He rose from the sofa with the doll in his hand, and went back down the steps and through the beaded curtain. As he was about to leave the shop, a woman called to him. "Excuse me sir. Are you gonna pay for that or do I need to call the police?"

He looked at the doll in his hand and replied, "Oh yeah, how much do I owe you?"

"That one'll be $12.95 plus tax." She half smiled, half glared at him.

"Yes, here you go." he handed her his credit card.

Back at the hotel, he sat on the bed holding the doll. It looked innocent enough, so maybe he just imagined what the man had said about it, he was pretty drunk when he went into the shop in the first place. He decided to put it in his suitcase and forget about it. In fact he laughed at how silly he was to be so apprehensive about a burlap doll filled with fluff.

The next day was occupied with some sightseeing and after another drunken night, a long drive home. The last day was spent getting back in the frame of mind to go back to work and face *The Beast*.

Monday morning came and James was at his desk early. After getting coffee, he began catching up on emails. When Hank arrived he was banging filing cabinet doors. "Hey man, what's up?" he spoke to the wall of his cubicle.

"Hey James! You're back! How was the vacay?" he came around to James cube.

"It was great!" he lied with the most enthusiasm he could muster. "I partied like it was 1995."

"Give me some deets, dude! You met some ladies?"

"Oh yeah, I think there were three, but it's a little bit fuzzy." He needed to change the subject. "So, anybody get fired while I was gone?"

"Wow, you aren't going to believe this James, man. Two days after you left, a friend of Renee's got wiped out in a car crash. Was mangled pretty bad from what I heard." He twisted himself up and stuck out his tongue to demonstrate. "Anyway, she has changed man. She came in on Friday and said she had been doing some *'soul searching'*, and she actually apologized for treating us like crap, for the last year."

"You're kidding me." James was feeling uncomfortable as he remembered what had happened in the voodoo shop.

"No man, it's true. In fact she scheduled a team lunch on Wednesday at that swanky restaurant uptown, what's it called? Oh yeah, Chops and Greens."

"Yeah, that's big. Well look man, I need to get ready for the meeting, so…"

"That's the other thing, no more weekly meetings. She switched it to monthly. Said something about empowering us more. Trust, and all that. But no problem, I know you need to get caught up. I'll slide."

"Yeah, we'll talk later. Thanks for the intel."

The rest of the day, thoughts of voodoo distracted him from his work. He even went on the web and researched. Everything he found though pointed to it being rooted in folklore of various cultures. By quitting time he had convinced himself he had nothing to worry about.

Renee called him into the office late on Monday and apologized to him in a special gesture that left him dumbfounded. He wondered how one friends death could have affected her so profoundly, but between then and now, she had been consistent in her new management style.

Wednesday came before he knew it. When it was time for lunch, he was getting ready to go alone when Cheryl intercepted him. "Come on James, Renee is buying lunch today." She smiled and took him by the arm. "You need to take advantage of something that isn't supposed to exist."

"What would that be?" He allowed himself to walk with her.

"A free lunch of course! You know how they always say there's…"

"No free lunch?" he finished the sentence.

"Yes, exactly!" and she pushed the button for the elevator.

At the restaurant, the whole team was gathered around the table talking and laughing. Some were looking at the menu, and others were looking for places to hang their jackets. As soon as everyone was settled, Renee stood and tapped her water glass with her fork.

"I'm glad everyone could make it today. I am sure some of you have been doubtful that what I said last week was true, and I wouldn't blame you if you did. To celebrate my new awakening I would encourage each of you to order anything from the menu that looks good. We are having wine with this meal, and then I am giving everyone the rest of the day off. Does anyone have any questions?"

Cheryl timidly raised her hand. "Uh, are we getting paid for it? I can't afford to take…"

Renee smiled wide, "Of course Cheryl, I think every…" she stopped mid word. And her face suddenly twisted into a painful grimace and turned bright red. Then her left arm shot out from her side as if someone had grabbed and yanked it. As the team watched in horror, a large cut opened up on her arm from her wrist to mid-bicep. It was as if she were being filleted. The gash opened wide to expose the bone and blood sprayed all over those sitting near her.

As quickly as the cutting stopped, her right arm detached from her body and flew across the room. It slammed into a large painting and knocked it off the wall to slam to the floor. Everyone was either screaming now or sitting with their jaws hanging open in shock. Blood sprayed from her shoulder as she shook from the violent assault on her body. Before she could pass out from pain, her left leg became detached, shot straight up to the ceiling, bounced off and landed on the table.

As Renee fell to the floor, her personal assistant obviously in shock, grabbed her leg from the table and desperately tried to push it back in place. She continued to try until the other one came off and slid across the floor at the feet of two women who were watching the whole thing in horror.

By now people were running from the restaurant screaming and hardly anyone noticed when her head came of cleanly, bounced a couple of times and landed upright on the stump of her severed neck. The only person left at the table was James. He was frozen in his seat. He knew what was happening. He was witnessing exactly what he had been told to do to the doll by the Jamaican guy.

Everything was quiet except for some sobbing in a corner. James stood from his chair and walked toward the bloody torso of Renee lying on the floor. As he stood staring, every piece of her burst into flame. He dropped to his knees and began to sob uncontrollably, but not because of what was happening in the room. It was because of what he knew he was now supposed to do.

As soon as everyone in the restaurant had been questioned by police, they were allowed to leave. James went back to his apartment, dragged himself up the stairs to his unit and when inside, collapsed onto the sofa. He stayed in that spot for the rest of the night. When he woke in the morning, he could not bring himself to leave.

He knew what he had to do, but he couldn't bring himself to get the doll from his closet and do it. He knew his time was running out. He kept remembering what he had been told. "There is no second try, no change of mind. You dismember and burn da image or you pay with you very soul." It rang in his ears over and over again.

He stayed in his apartment for the next three days. When the phone rang he ignored it. It was on the morning of the fourth day that he talked himself into doing what he had been told to do. He went to the closet and fetched the doll. Then he got a pair of scissors from the kitchen drawer and went to sit on the sofa. He had a tight grip on the torso of the doll in one hand. "Please forgive me." He said out loud as he opened the scissors to cut. Then he felt a sharp pain in his leg. As he watched in horror, a jagged wound opened at the top of his thigh. It was as if someone were sawing through his leg to remove it from his body and they had cut straight through his jeans to do it! He could feel the jagged edge of a blade as it cut. As the main artery was severed, he felt the life spraying from his body. There was nothing he could do. The leg fell to the floor and the cutting moved to his arm. He was being dismembered and he only had seconds to live.

As his arm fell to the floor, James screamed and passed out with terror frozen in his mind. Not because of the pain as he was being butchered, but at the thought of the loss of his soul, *his very soul.*

Horror Challenge Topics: Frog and Tiara
Suggested by: Ruthi Kight and MaryAnn Inabinet
RMFabBookReviews.blogspot.com

TO KISS A FROG

Danika was like a lot of ten-year-old girls. For as long as she could remember, she had dreamed of being a princess. She had many costumes and accessories for pretending, but she was coming to an age when she had other interests. Boys specifically.

When she was younger, what had bothered her most about being a princess was the whole prince thing. After all, boys were disgusting, weren't they? They were always getting dirty, fighting, and doing mean things to her and her friends. If that wasn't bad enough, they often wandered over to bother her and her friends. Frequently, it would lead to being chased around her yard while the boy threatened her with some disgusting creature.

Now, she was old enough to see boys in a different light. In the stories about princesses, sometimes the girl would kiss a frog and he would turn into a handsome prince. If only that were true, she could have her prince and bypass all the nasty things about boys.

When Danika's brother Todd came home from college during summer vacation, she helped him unload his stuff and carry it up to his room. As he put his things away, she sat cross-legged on the bed and talked to him about school. She told him all about her friends and, to her surprise, he told her about his new girlfriend. It was fascinating to hear how he talked about the girl he was dating, a Brazilian girl. It seemed she knew a lot of history about her country.

Danika had missed her brother. She had always enjoyed having him around and now she was contributing more than her share to the conversation, but when he unpacked the small glass aquarium holding a large green frog, she went wide-eyed with curiosity.

"Is that a frog? It's huge!" She put her face up against the glass and watched the frog turn to look into her eyes. "He looks friendly enough. What kind of frog is he?"

Todd laughed at his sister making faces at his pet and finally replied, "He's a magical frog."

Danika gasped. "Really? Is that what they really call him, magical?"

"Well, he's a Colorado River toad, but he's kind of magical."

"What do you mean?" She started lifting the lid of the aquarium.

"Don't touch him!" Todd sounded panicked.

"Why can't I touch him?" She quickly set the lid back down as though he had hurt her feelings.

Now what? He couldn't exactly tell her that he and his friends used this green toad to get stoned. Nor was he going to explain that if you squeezed it just right the liquid it secreted was hallucinogenic. *Oh yeah, Dannie*, he thought, *it's just like being on acid. Right!* That is not something that you want to tell your little sister.

Instead, he simply said, "Uh, well, you know how those stories go? The princess kisses the frog, and he turns into a prince? No way do I want Bart turning into a prince. He'd break his tank if he grew that fast, and I'd lose my pet.

Besides, what would we do with a prince?" He laughed. "Go on now. I want to go see the gang before it gets too late."

Danika looked as though he had slapped her. "Todd, I wasn't going to kiss him! I just wanted to hold him for a minute."

"Not a good idea. Look, I'm gonna go hang out with my friends for a while. Maybe when I get home I'll take him out and you can watch him eat. Now get going, I need to change my clothes." He chased her out of the room and got dressed to go out.

About an hour later, she was watching a show on the TV when it came to her. Since no one was home, it wouldn't hurt if she went and just looked at the frog. She might even pick it up if she dared. Through the bay window, she checked the driveway to see if Todd's car was there before running upstairs to his room.

The bedroom was dark except for the light in the aquarium, which lit up the dresser around it. She flipped on the light and walked over to peer in at the olive green reptile through the glass. She hadn't noticed the golden dots covering its skin when she had looked at it earlier.

"Hey, Bart," she called to it in her sweetest voice. "Todd says you're a magical frog. Is that for reals?"

The toad merely looked at her and blinked its eyes.

"You can understand me, can't you? Blink if you know what I'm saying."

The toad blinked again.

Danika was excited now. It actually understood her. She had to find out if it really was a magical frog. She went to the window and checked again for Todd's car. Satisfied, she returned to remove the mesh lid from the tank and reached in to grab hold of Bart. He was sitting very still until she lifted him from the tank. Slimier than she had expected, he easily jumped from her hands and landed on the carpet with a 'thunk'.

Now she was panicked. The toad was jumping around on the floor while she scrambled and tried to catch it. No sooner would she get her hands around it, than he would slip from her grasp again. Over and over, she tried to catch him. Before she knew it, the slimy secretions from the toad were all over her hands. At last, she managed to hold him in her grip and get him back into the tank. She closed the lid with a sigh of relief.

Danika was glad to put him safely back where he belonged, but she was beginning to feel strange. There were colors waving around the ceiling light and the room seemed to sway as she stood there leaning against Todd's dresser. Bart was looking at her through the tank and that was when he spoke to her. "I'm hungry, Princess. Could you bring me something to eat?"

She went a little cross-eyed as she looked at him more closely. "Did you just talk?"

"I'd like a sandwich," the frog replied.

"He just asked me to make him a sandwich!" She smiled to nobody there. Giggling, she said back to him, "Yes, my lord."

Curtsying like one of the princesses she saw in a movie, Danika headed down to the kitchen. She was having trouble with the stairs, so she got down on her hands and knees to crawl down backwards. When her foot touched the floor at the bottom, she turned and wobbled into the kitchen.

The lights seemed so bright and the colors much more intense here. She squinted as she looked around. Why was she here? She couldn't remember. "Oh yes, a sandwich," she said. Without a thought about the slime on her hands, she opened the refrigerator. Pulling out a plate of leftover ham, she set it on the counter. Bread, mayo, and tomatoes, soon she had all of the ingredients. Leaving the refrigerator door open wide, she was ready to make the sandwich if only she could get the room to stop spinning.

Her stomach was hurting, and she guessed that she must be hungry, too. She put a piece of ham in her mouth and chewed it. Pretty good, she thought as she swallowed, but making the sandwich was another story. No matter how she tried, the ham would not go onto the bread. She even tried pressing it into the bread, but it curled up and yelled at her. "No!" It startled her so much that she ended up dropping it on the floor. And, forget trying to get the lid off the mayonnaise jar. The whole thing slipped out of her hands and fell on the floor rolling away. "Darn!"

Suddenly, the whole thing struck her as funny. Sliding down to the floor with her back to the cupboard, Danika laughed so hard she thought her chest would open right up. When she tried to stand up again, she did not have any feeling in her legs. She grabbed hold of the cabinet door handle to pull herself up, but instead she managed to open it. She let out a gasp.

Inside the cupboard was the most beautiful diamond tiara she had ever seen! She must have it. Her head was reeling as she reached in and pulled out the metal spaghetti strainer. She hugged it to her breast for a moment as she received the applause and cheers of all the people she imagined around her. With a tip of her head, she put it on.

She was so happy. Now she had everything any princess could want. Her loyal subjects, a prince who was waiting upstairs, and now she had this beautiful tiara. Too bad her stomach was hurting, and the colors drifting down from the light were so thick. They swirled like strokes of paint around her.

Was she scared? She laughed at that. She had so many friends here with her. She just needed to sit for a minute. Somehow, she got to her knees and crawled into the family room where the TV was still on. It was so beautiful! The dog on the screen seemed to be running through heaven, and then it jumped right out of the television and onto the sofa.

"Nice... dog... Good... dog," she managed to say as she pulled herself onto the sofa to sit down with the dog, but it was gone! "Doggie..." she rasped as she straightened her tiara and leaned back. She was tired. She needed to rest for a minute.

A few hours later, her mother came home from work. She came in through the kitchen carrying groceries and found the bread and ham out on the counter along with the unopened jar of mayonnaise on the floor. The television was playing in the next room. She called out, "Dannie? Are you okay?" There was no answer. "Dannie?"

She took up a large knife from the wooden block on the counter and crept slowly into the family room. As she came around the sofa, she saw her daughter sitting slumped on the sofa, a spaghetti strainer tangled in her hair. There was a trail of vomit down the front of her shirt, but Danika did not move. Her mother screamed trying desperately to revive her lifeless daughter.

Just then, Todd returned home and ran to his sister, pushing his mother aside as she continued to scream. "No, Dannie!" "Call 911!" he yelled. It didn't take long to guess what had happened. He lifted Danika's eyelids as he patted her cheek, then he checked for a pulse but he couldn't feel it.

"Please, Dannie, wake up!" Why hadn't he told her the truth about the excretions from the toad's skin? It was a psychedelic substance, but very poisonous. Maybe then, she wouldn't have touched it. "I'm so sorry!" Todd began to sob uncontrollably.

Unfortunately, he never knew that his sister had been overwhelmed with a desire to fulfill the dream she had carried for most of her young life, to kiss a frog.

Horror Challenge Topic: Hummingbird
Suggested by: Brittany Carrigan
Thecoverbybrittany.blogspot.com

A Garden Secret

Madeline loved her backyard garden. It was easy to see how much pride she took in every display of color, especially her rose bushes. Although she had never entered any competition, she often said that her roses were prize winning. They were stunning. Every summer, she invited friends for afternoon tea, just to show off her flowers.

One beautiful Saturday morning, she was out in the garden again, fertilizing and pulling weeds. As was her typical routine, she began on one side and methodically worked her way around to the other side, taking care to inspect and improve every inch of the rich black soil that made everything grow so well.

She was nearly finished for the day when she looked back over her work and caught a glimpse of something she hadn't noticed before. It was some sort of container with strange markings on it. If she had to describe it, she wouldn't have called it a box, a bottle, or even a cylinder. It was an oddly shaped item to be sure. How she could have worked this soil only a short while ago and not have seen it?

"What in the world? Where did this come from?" she asked aloud to nobody there as she bent to pull the thing from the ground. It was partially embedded as though it had been there for some time. "How could that be?" she wondered. She wrapped her gloved hand around it to pull it out. The thing began to buzz or maybe it was a vibration. Startled, she let go of it. Rather than use her hands, she decided to dig it out with a shovel. She would have to go through the door at the back of the garage to fetch one.

Madeline entered the garage just in time to hear the phone ringing in the house. Her mouth twisted in frustration as she walked through the door that led to the kitchen through the laundry room, removing her dirty gloves as she went. She managed to catch the phone on the fourth ring. "Hello, this is Madeline," she answered, forcing a cheerful voice.

"Hi, Mads!" the equally cheerful voice on the line greeted her. She immediately recognized her friend, Carol. "What are you up to on this beautiful afternoon? I bet you were working in the garden, right?"

"Yes, I was. You know me so well." She walked over to the window so she could look out at the object. She could still see it sticking up out of the ground. "As a matter of fact, right now I am looking out my window at all the beautiful color."

"I bet it's gorgeous on a day like this."

"Indeed, it is. It's the strangest thing, though. I found something odd out amongst the flowers. You might think me crazy, but it looks almost... alien?"

There was a slight hesitation, and then the sound of Carol's unbridled laughter came ringing out of the phone. "Really, Mads, I just love your sense of humor! That's why I called to see if you wanted to go shopping at the plaza later. I thought maybe we could get a bite and..."

"No, Carol. I'm not kidding. I found something out there and, believe me, I've been working that dirt for years, and I've never seen anything like this before." She swallowed hard. "Tell you what. Come on over in… let's say, an hour and a half. I'll dig it out and show you. Then we can go to dinner and shop."

"Okay then. See you around five."

"Right. Bye now." Madeline was eager to get back to the garden. She went back to the garage, put her gloves back on, got her shovel, and then back to the garden she went. For some reason she had felt a little panicked, as if the object might be gone when she returned, but a sense of relief washed over her as she found it right where she had left it.

Careful not to crush any of her flowers, she placed the tip of the shovel against the object and pushed it down with her foot. Lifting the object up and out, it fell away from the dirt as clean as though it had been washed. It was about a foot long and cylindrical in the shape of some kind of missile made of some kind of shiny metal. The end that had been buried in the ground was turned with threads like a screw.

Madeline slid the shovel further under it to lift it out of the flowerbed. It was heavier than she expected. She moved her hands toward the metal head of the shovel and tried again. This time it was easier to lift, and she carried it to the center of the grassy area between the beds and laid it on the ground. She got down on her hands and knees to get a closer look.

It was a work of beauty, smooth and iridescent in the light of the sun. She turned her ear to make out whether the quiet hum she heard was indeed emanating from within the peculiar object. Oddly, she found the sound to be quite soothing.

Without warning, one end of the object began to turn, twisting itself off the cylinder. A full two inches of the flattened end, fell off onto the ground. She was spellbound. Part of her wanted to run away, but the other part wondered what would happen next. A few seconds later, she had her answer.

Madeline saw only a blur, and then she heard a low buzzing noise. The thing took off across her garden, weaving in and out of the flowers the way that a bee might, but this was no bee. A small body, rapid wing movements, and long needlelike beak... Were those legs with feet on them hanging underneath?

Captivated by the flashes of changing color as it flitted about, she followed it with her gaze. It must be some kind of hummingbird, she thought. In a moment, the thing was hovering only inches from her face. "You are a strange little creature." She spoke quietly so as not to scare it away. Before her eyes, the tiny bird-like creature cycled through a range of the most beautiful colors she had ever seen. "Strange to be sure, but beautiful." Almost as though responding to her words, the creature buzzed in a rhythm with her voice as she spoke. "I think I'll call you Buzzby." She smiled. "But what are you?"

Just as her lips formed the last word of her question, the thing flew straight into her mouth. She let out a squeal of surprise, but there was no chance to spit it out. It braced itself against her tongue and drove the sharp spike of its beak straight through the roof of her mouth directly into her brain.

She could make no more than a muffled sound as the Buzzby blocked her mouth and rapidly extended its beak to a full three feet. It quickly curled through her skull and entwined itself in her brain. When she fell face first into the dirt, Buzzby was stunned for a moment and was forced to regain his footing inside her mouth. He was in the process of surgically connecting her neurons to his consciousness.

The fall jarred his concentration, and he no longer had the control he required. The plump creature he was working on was lying on the ground, jerking and twitching, and that was not what he had intended. He needed to take control so he could begin his feeding. It had been so very long since he had eaten. With a great deal of mental focus, Buzzby finally located the creature's control center. As the body relaxed, its mouth opened allowing the warm light to shine in. At last, it had stopped moving.

Wasting no time, he began sucking on the fluids that were seeping down along his long proboscis. He vibrated to keep a constant flow. Once he began to feel somewhat satisfied, he realized that something was happening that he wasn't expecting. Small bumps were cropping up all over his body. At the same time, his hunger returned. The more nourishment he took in, the larger the bumps became.

In minutes, the bumps were so large that he felt his body filling up the small space he currently occupied. He shuddered. Suddenly, the bumps exploded all at once, and Buzzby was dead. Collapsed inside the host creature's mouth, his limp body was buffeted by tiny wings as more than a hundred Buzzby clones struggled to free themselves from the cramped space. As they reached the opening, they flew to freedom and spread out across the landscape.

Next door, a woman stood on her back porch calling her dog when the tiny colorful creature flew into her mouth. Seconds later, she tumbled down the steps to land crumpled on the sidewalk below. Two houses down in the other direction, three children were playing on their backyard gym. They were chasing each other and laughing when the small group of 'bugs' invaded their bodies. One little girl screamed just before she collapsed, which brought her mother out to see what was wrong. The woman yelled and fell next to her kids where she lay helpless and twitching on the ground.

Madeline's friend, Carol had decided to leave her house early. As she pulled up in front of her friend's house, she noticed the man across the street lying in the grass next to his running lawn mower. She started over to help the man but, when she saw his condition, she decided it would be better to call 911 and get help right away. When she got to Madeline's front door, she loudly pounded on it with her fist. Unwilling to wait for an answer, she tried the doorknob. The door swung open.

Carol ran in calling out to her friend, but there was no one to be found. From the corner of her eye, she saw the phone and hurried to dial for help. The dispatcher asked, "911, what's your emergency?" Carol told her about the man across the street, gave Madeline's address as a reference, and hung up the phone. She wondered what could have happened to Madeline. Surely she was around here somewhere, maybe in the garden.

She would go out there just as soon as she got herself a drink. There was a full pitcher of filtered water sitting right in front of her on the counter, and her anxiety had made her extremely thirsty. Probably, Madeline needed a drink as well if she was still out in the garden. She opened the cabinet above the sink and took out two glasses, then poured some water from the pitcher. Just as she put one of the glasses to her lips, a small colorful bug tumbled into the water unnoticed. Hearing sirens, she went to the front window in time to see the ambulance pulling up across the street. She watched as the paramedics got out and ran to the man.

Relieved, she took a long sip of the cool water. No sooner did she swallow than she felt a pain in her stomach. A long needlelike object began to poke through her sweater.

It stretched out in front of her nearly six inches. A small spot of red started to spread across her belly as she watched in horror. Panicked, she ran out of the house toward the paramedics. As she rounded the ambulance, she found them convulsing on the ground next to the man. She was so frightened she let out a scream. Another 'bug' took advantage of the opportunity and flew into her mouth. It quickly sent her tumbling to the ground.

All through the neighborhood, the cloud of death was spreading. The tiny colorful creatures flew and people fell. It happened so quickly, no one could send out a warning. By the next morning, the sprawling city fell quiet. Bodies littered the streets, and a colorful cloud of tiny creatures drifted across the countryside growing larger by the minute.

No one in their path was warned. They only heard the buzz.

Horror Challenge Topic: A Story of Historical Fiction
Suggested by: AO Bibliophile
aobibliosphere.blogspot.com

JUST ADD WATER

In the last years of slavery, a Spanish slave ship named
Trouvadore made land in São Tomé, a Portuguese colony
off the coast of Africa. The year was 1841. When the ship
again set sail, their cargo manifest included some treasures of
gold, artifacts from the region and 280 slaves. This is their
fateful story.

The natives from the kingdom of Kongo had been
brought to the island weeks earlier after being captured by
roving bands of slavers. They were awaiting a ship from
Spain whose purpose was to transport the captives to Cuba.
There they would be put to work on the Cuban sugar cane
plantations.

Two weeks into captivity, this group was proven to be
defiant. Led by the Priestess from one of the villages where
the captives had lived, an uprising threatened to destroy the
operations on the small island. The ruler of the island,
Armando De Principe, gave the command that any dissident
within the population found to be causing trouble must be
executed and burned in view of the other captives. An
example was to be made in order to regain control, and this
would achieve the desired result.

On a clear night in the midst of unrest, the Priestess was
detained. A bonfire was built from fallen palm trees and
driftwood gathered from the beach. The captives were

forced to watch as their Priestess was bound and thrown into the flames. In her dying moments, she screamed out a curse in a language her captors could not understand.

"When the ship is near the island, my ashes will revenge. Your people will perish and mine will be set free!" she chanted as the flesh burned from her bones and all fell silent. In the early hours of the following morning, a few of her villagers collected her ashes in a clay jar and hid them among the cargo that was to accompany the slaves when all were loaded into the ship. The captors had achieved their goal and there were no more protests.

When the slave ship Trouvadore arrived at the island days later, supplies, cargo, and the African slaves were loaded without incident, and the ship set sail for Cuba. In the weeks that followed, the Trouvadore was beset by rough seas and though the crew had made this trip several times before, they began to believe that they were cursed. Several times they found themselves hundreds of miles off course. There was talk of mutiny, but the men feared the consequences of that action more than the tribulations they were enduring.

Disease and starvation began to take a toll on the captives who were locked below deck. Each day the dead were carried up the ladder into the sunlight and thrown unceremoniously from the back of the ship. For weeks, the scene was repeated, and the crew and their human cargo became increasingly concerned that none of them would reach their destination.

One calm and starry night, as they were finally sailing up the coast of South America, a few of the captives were awakened by the sound of chanting rising up from the deck below. When they ventured down to investigate, they were startled to find the ghost of their Priestess standing there upon a crate.

She turned her eyes toward them and commanded, "From within this crate, take the jar of my ashes into the depths of the ship. Empty them into the bilge water. Prepare to be free, and cast into the sea." Immediately, the ghost vanished.

The frightened men fell over each other as they climbed back up the ladder to their deck. Questioned by their elders, they told what they had seen and heard. After a brief discussion, the order went out to secure their quarters, to find anything on the lower levels of the ship that might float and have it at the ready when the time came.

The elders descended into the depths of the ship led by one of the men who had received the instructions of the Priestess. He directed them to the appropriate shipping crate. When the crate was opened, the clay jar was carefully removed. Two elders were chosen to carry the ashes to the lowest level of the ship, while the others went up to prepare their people for whatever was to come next.

In the bowels of the ship, the elders stood looking down at the bilge water that stood in the bottom of the ship. With a nod to one another, the one who held the jar carefully removed the lid and stepped closer to the dark water. Looking back toward the other, he poured the ashes into the water. They stood for a moment watching, and then there was movement on the water. What began as a ripple in the surface was soon followed by the shape of a creature resembling the Priestess rising up to appear before them. Although this beast had large curved claws and long spikes running along its spine, the face was unmistakably that of their Priestess.

She let out a fierce growl before leaping to the side of the ship just above the water, grasping the wooden beams with her sharp claws. With a howl, she dug into one of the beams and, tore it from the others in a show of incredible strength. The seawater rushed in with a roar as the elders scrambled up the ladder. Terrible sounds of the howling creature blended into the shattering of timber behind them. Within minutes, the ship would be going down.

On deck, the captain noticed as the ship began to shake and shudder. He ordered five of his men to go below and seek out the cause of the strange vibrations. Upon unchaining and opening the hatch, they were met by a rush of their captives, pouring out from the deck below.

They pushed their way up, overwhelming the crew, many of whom were asleep at their posts.

When the ship sank, everyone was thrown into the water. One hundred and ninety slaves and fifty members of the crew all thrashed and struggled to find some object to float on. Suddenly, something below the water and out of view began to pull each member of the crew beneath the surface. One by one, they screamed as an unseen beast grabbed and pulled them under. Not one of them resurfaced.

All but a few of the slaves found something from the ship to help them stay afloat, and the ones who were left to swim on their own claimed later that some unknown force had kept their heads above water. Certain their time had come to an end, they called out to one another as they waited in the darkness hoping for a miracle.

At dawn, a British ship headed out from the Turks and Caicos Islands, came upon the slaves floating in the sea. The crew pulled the hapless survivors from the water, considering them hysterical as they carried on about a creature that had sunk their ship.

Once on land, the captives were relieved to find that they had been taken to a British colony where slavery had been abolished years earlier. Descendents of those slaves remain on the islands to this very day, and the story continues to pass from father to son of the Priestess who gave her life so they might all be saved from slavery and the sea.

Footnote: Although this tale is based on a true story, to this day it is not known what caused the ship to sink on calm seas in the middle of the night. Reportedly, the crew did not drown, but survived, were put on trial and convicted on charges related to slavery.

Horror Challenge Topic: Library & Letter Opener
Suggested by: Jennifer & Marty of Fictitiousmusings.com

THE LETTER "L"

Thirteen year-old Lori loved her books. So much so, she would just as soon read as do anything else. She spent hours shut away in her room, day after day, doing just that. One can imagine, therefore, how it must have surprised her mother when she said that she would be attending her friend's party on Halloween. Even more surprising was that Lori planned to trick-or-treat with the kids from the party in her friend's neighborhood. Though taken off guard, Lori's mom hoped that her bookworm daughter might actually begin to make friends and have some kind of a social life.

On the afternoon of Halloween, Lori's mother presented her with a costume she had put together with some left over fabric from one of her sewing projects. It was a white robe with angel wings attached to the back with pins and a halo made with glittery pipe cleaners. Even though it was handmade, it was a nice costume, and her mother was confident that Lori would be comfortable wearing it to the party.

At three o'clock, Lori announced that it was time to go, and her father loaded her into the car and drove her to the party. In front of her friend's house, Lori jumped out of the car with her costume and a jacket in her arms. Closing the door with her hip, she said goodbye and thanked her dad.

"You sure you don't need help getting in the house with all that stuff?" he offered.

"No, dad, I'm fine," she said. Over her shoulder she
added, "Lucy's mom is gonna bring me home around
eleven." She turned and walked slowly up the sidewalk to the
porch.

When she was sure her dad's Buick had turned the
corner, she stopped and laid her jacket on the ground. She
rolled the costume into a ball and tied the sleeves of her
jacket into a makeshift knapsack, then stuffed the costume
into it and hung it over her shoulder. Lucy just happened to
live three blocks from the library, and it only took Lori ten
minutes to skip over there. She had never planned to go to a
party, but to spend her evening reading scary stories written
by her favorite authors, Edgar Allen Poe and Ann Radcliff.

This would be a very special evening, for she would be
doing what she loved most, and reading the very stories that
had earned her mother's stern disapproval. To her, this was
just as daring an act as soaping windows or putting a paper
bag full of dog poop on somebody's porch and lighting it on
fire. Lori had been told that the fun in that act was watching
the horrified homeowner trying to stomp out the fire, but
she doubted the entertainment value of it. She thought her
friends silly for being involved in things like that. It was the
neighborhood boys who always talked them into it. Those
boys were nothing but trouble, and she stayed as far from
them as she could.

As she stepped through the doors of the library, the
familiar smell of books rushed out at her. Surely, this is what
heaven must smell like, she thought as she headed straight to
a table to abandon her jacket and the costume wrapped in it.
Within minutes, she was sitting at her favorite table reading
by the light of the green shaded lamp.

She savored the tales of Poe, the dark poetry of his words
and shivered as she imagined the beating of the telltale heart

directly behind her. Before she knew it, the old lady librarian announced, "The library is closing early due to Halloween. Please finish making your selections. The library will open again at ten tomorrow morning."

This can't be, thought Lori, looking at the clock on the wall. The time was seven o'clock, and she had planned to stay until at least nine when the library normally closed. This was a travesty! Her young mind churned in an effort to decide what to do next. Her eyes fell upon the sign to the ladies' room. A light bulb must have surely appeared above her head as the answer came to her. She would hide in a stall in the bathroom until everyone was gone, and then come out and read until almost ten o'clock. Afterward, she could go back to Lucy's house and ask her mom for a ride home. Lucy's mom was very nice, and Lori was sure her dad wouldn't mind if she got a ride. She already knew what she would say to explain why she was out so late.

With her plan worked out in her head, she marked her place in the book and stacked it and the others on a chair. Pushing the pile out of sight under the table, she snuck into the bathroom and settled into a stall. She locked the door, sat down on the toilet, and pulled up her feet. The library was large and sound carried well, so when the librarian left, the sound of the door locking behind her drifted in to Lori. She slowly pushed open the door to the restroom, peeping out to be certain the coast was clear. Finally satisfied, she stepped out into the vacant library.

"Mine, all mine!" she exclaimed holding out her arms as if she were trying to hold every book in view. She was so excited by the prospect of being alone in such a wonderful place that she skipped around the tables, touching the backs of the chairs as she went. From there, she began skipping past the rows of books. Starting at A and calling out the letters as she went, "B, C... H, I, J, K..." Just as the letter L was about to escape her lips, a very large man stepped directly in her path. Unable to stop, she crashed into him.

"Hey!" the man exclaimed, "You not s'pose to be here."

Lori had never before encountered Lloyd, the mentally disabled janitor, and did not realize that the library was cleaned each night after hours. She quickly picked herself up off the floor, scrambling backward as he reached for her with his dirty hands. Frightened, she turned and ran.

"You. Stop!" he repeatedly called after her as she frantically headed for the door. He was only steps behind her as she desperately tried to open it. She ducked just out of his grasp, as he tried to stop and slammed against the door. She ran to the librarian's desk and ducked under it, grabbing a silver letter opener from the desktop that was lying out in the open.

Lloyd did not see where she had gone, so he began looking around trying to find her. He was on his knees checking under a table when he caught sight of her dress through the gap below the front of the librarian's desk. Loudly he sighed as he ambled over to the desk and reached down to feel around for her. Lori sucked in her breath as she pulled back and determinedly stabbed his arm with the letter opener.

Enraged from pain, he howled and leapt toward her, as she tried to scurry away from his grasp. He caught hold of her foot, tripping her, and watched helplessly as she seemed to fall in slow motion, her head striking the card catalog cabinet. By the time he regained his footing and bent to check on her, she was already dead. Her neck had snapped as clean as a cheap wooden pencil in the fall.

Lloyd got down on his knees and nudged her, hoping she would get up, but she didn't move. "Wake up!" he said as he tried again. Panic swept over him, and he looked to the phone trying to decide whether to call someone. Instead, he swept her up in his arms and carried her over to a door marked 'Boiler Room'. As he swung the door open, he muttered to himself, "Lloyd in big trouble. Gotta hide."

Down the steps, he carried Lori's lifeless body, to look for somewhere to hide her. On the other side of the room, a door with a glass panel glowed from the fire within, spreading its orange light across the floor. It was the incinerator, and he had fired it up to burn the trash only a half hour before. Now it was burning hot, and he pondered a long moment before deciding what he must do.

He carried the girl over and threw open the door to the incinerator. With tears running down his cheeks, he looked down at the girl in his arms. "I sorry," he said, beginning to weep, as he slid her through the opening and closed the door. Lloyd stood watching through the glass as her hair melted and her cotton dress caught fire, then turned away and slumped to the floor crying over what he had done.

What remained of Lori was discovered the next morning when the librarian opened for the day. There was a strange smell about the place and, right away, she had noticed the blood on the floor next to the letter opener, but the janitor was never to be found.

Every Halloween since that horrific event, Lori's spirit was cursed to relive her untimely demise. Tonight, for the sixty-second time, the life faded from her as she lay on the cold library floor. A final thought passed through her mind as it had that fateful night, "Maybe it's better to burn a bag of poop on somebody's porch after all."

Horror Challenge Topic: Mailman.
Suggested by: Delphina
DelphinaReadsTooMuch.com

OVERNIGHT DELIVERY

Sam the mailman hated Halloween. It wasn't so much the day itself, because it was just another day. No, the problem for him was the whole costumes and decorations thing. The other problem was the kids.

This Halloween, he had spent the day being chased by agitated dogs, dodging fake spider webs, and tripping over jack-o-lanterns. Now that his shift was over and all of his mail delivered, he was trying to make his way back to the post office.

He was carefully watching for kids excited by the prospects of going out right after dark. On this day of the year they were careless in the streets. Last year he had almost run one over, and he wasn't going to deal with that hassle again. As far as he was concerned there was nothing worse than panicked, screaming parents.

So you might imagine, after the slow drive back to the office, he was relieved to park his truck and carry the empty mail trays in before going home. When he stepped through the door, his supervisor, Dan was waiting for him.

"Hey Sam, I'm glad you're back. I have this overnight delivery that has to go out, and you're the first one back. I need you to take it."

Sam was disheartened by this announcement. He expected to be on his way home in a few minutes. He had to think fast, "Yeah you know I would take it, but that would be overtime and you know what they said about overtime. No way." He smiled thinking he had avoided the situation with his clever response.

"Overtime is it? Well, that's no problem, we can give you that." Dan replied shoving the package into Sam's hands.

Now Sam could feel the anger rising. "But I had p-p-plans..." Sam stuttered trying to wriggle out of the situation.

"You going trick or treating tonight, Sam?"

He shook his head no.

"Oh that's right, you don't have kids do you? Well, I figure since you live on Oak Street, this delivery is on your way home. Just leave your uniform on and you can drop it on your way. The address is Maple Street, you won't even have to make a turn to deliver it."

"Maple Street?" Sam inquired. Suddenly it didn't seem all that bad. "What about the overtime?"

"No problemo, buddy." Dan smiled, "I'll sign for an extra hour, how's that sound?"

Reluctantly, Sam nodded in agreement, and Dan scurried off to the front of the building. By the time Sam had put everything in its place, Dan was already gone. "He could have dropped it off." He muttered under his breath as he headed to his car.

On Maple Street, he drove slowly looking for house numbers, and again was very careful about the kids walking around in their costumes. The little buggers were already out. He'd wanted to be home before they got started.

Eventually he found the address, a large old gray house with a 'For Sale' sign out front. Cars were parked up and down the street, but he managed to find a space and pulled in. As he walked to the door carrying the package, it didn't look like anyone was home. There were no lights shining through the windows.

He knocked and counted to five then knocked again. He looked at the package while he waited and noticed the special instructions on the shipping label. "Do not leave."

"Man, what the f…" he almost got the word out when the door swung open. Standing before him was a beautiful dark haired woman dressed in some kind of a costume. Her robe was long and velvety and she wore a mask that covered only her eyes.

"There you are, just in time, come on in." She grabbed his forearm and dragged him through the door.

The house was lit on the inside by what must have been hundreds of candles and the light from them cast a warm glow on the other people in the house. It looked like they were getting ready for a party, and the best part of it for Sam, it was all women.

There were five beautiful ones to be exact, and all of them were dressed in exotic robed costumes with similar types of masks. He smiled in spite of himself, what had Dan gotten him into? Whatever it was he made a mental note to thank his boss in the morning.

Just then one of the women asked "Would you like some punch?" she waved her arm toward a punch bowl resting on a table near the wall.

"I… ah, need to get going." Sam began, but then he thought about this situation and quickly changed his mind, "Oh why not, just one."

No sooner had the words left his lips, he had a glass cup shoved into his hand. "Drink up cutie." The woman whispered to him in a sexy voice, "Let's get the party started."

That was all the encouragement he needed. He chugged the wonderfully fruity punch as fast as he could swallow, "That's good. That's really good." he said handing the empty cup back to the woman.

"I'm glad you like it." She smiled, "It takes me hours to make that potion." She winked and turned, then left the room.

It was at that moment that Sam noticed - no one else was drinking. Quicker than an ice cube on a hot iron skillet, he melted to the floor and was swallowed by darkness.

Minutes before midnight, he was awakened by pressure on his chest and something cold and wet on his face. The woman who was straddling his chest was saying, "Wakey, Wakey." She stood to join the others as he regained consciousness. He slowly turned his head from side to side and became aware that he couldn't move his arms or legs.

"What the hell is going on, where am i?" He asked frantically hoping someone would laugh and tell him this was just a prank.

He couldn't see the large black plastic mat that had been laid on the floor beneath him. Nor could he see the circle and the star inside of it that his body had been laid on. What he could see was several more people than had been present earlier and they included men in hooded black robes. These people were gathered in a circle around him and were looking down at him as they began to chant words he was not familiar with.

Suddenly, a gap opened in the crowd and another man stepped forward holding the box he had delivered to them earlier. He opened the box and reached inside, pulling a long jagged edged dagger from it. Then he reached up and pulled the hood from his head exposing his face.

"Dan?" Sam said puzzled at seeing his boss holding the dagger. "I get it, this is a joke…" He laughed nervously, "Untie me, man."

His boss wasn't smiling, "I'm sorry Sam, not a joke my friend. We are indeed very serious, and you delivered just the package we needed to arrive tonight – regardless of rain, hail, snow nor gloom of night."

"What the hell are you talking about Dan, untie me!" His eyes were growing wider with fear.

"I'm talking about you, Sam. You were the package I needed delivered." Those were the last words he spoke in English as he knelt next to his screaming co worked and thrust the dagger into his chest.

Blood spilled down Sam's side as Dan sawed through his sternum and reached in to pull the still beating heart from his chest. With a shriek, he held it over his head and squeezed it until it stopped throbbing and shooting blood from the torn arteries.

Outside the house, all was quiet. The neighborhood kids were at home trying to sleep through their sugar buzz, and no one heard the screaming coming from inside.

When the sun came up the next morning, everyone was gone. There was no sign of the gathering that had been held in this vacant home. Sam was gone, his body having been disposed of carefully, no trace of him would ever be found. Since he had no family, he would also never be missed.

At the post office, the drivers were headed out on their routes. Dan was going over some instructions with a new mail carrier. The man had been promoted from previously being a relief driver, to a full time position.

"So this is a map of your route. Half of your load is already sorted for you, the other half will be waiting for you here after lunch." He handed the keys for the mail truck to the new guy. "One other question…"

"Yeah, what's that?" The new guy took the keys from his hand.

"You don't have a problem with overtime do you?"

"Nah, I can use the extra cash." He said as he headed to his truck.

Dan smiled and nodded as he walked to his desk whistling a happy tune. Today was a new day and he was feeling younger and better than he had for months.

Horror Challenge Topic: The Boogeyman under the bed.
Suggested by: Katie Dalton
www.ISmellSheep.com

KITTY UNDER THE BED

Kayla was huddled under her covers with the flashlight again. Even though it was warm in her room, she had refused to open the window as her Dad had suggested. She just didn't know what monsters there might be about this close to Halloween, and she wasn't about to take a chance to find out.

If she was lucky, she might be able to get some sleep tonight. Maybe she would fall asleep before she might hear the sounds she had been hearing every night for the last few days. It was the sounds of something breathing and growling softly and even though she had told her Mom about it, Dad said she had to sleep in her room.

"It's just the sound of the bed creaking when you move." He said, "That is surely nothing to be afraid of."

"But Dad, I don't think I was moving." She argued in futility.

Nevertheless, he and Mom had gotten into an argument when she suggested that perhaps, just until after Halloween that Kayla might sleep in the room with them. Ultimately Dad had won the argument, and here she was sweating and listening to every creak in the old house from her safe haven under the blankets.

Suddenly she heard a creaking sound that made her jump and the light switch was flipped to reveal the lump of a girl hiding in her bed.

"Kayla Marie, what on earth are you doing under there?" Her Mom didn't sound mad, she just was asking in her normal voice. Sheepishly, Kayla pulled the blankets down to reveal herself.

"Oh, hi Mom. I was sleeping, what time is it?"

from behind her mother, Kitty ran through the doorway and in a single leap, landed on the bed beside Kayla. The cat began rubbing itself back and forth on her leg until she reached down and started petting it.

"Listen honey, I know you are scared, but there's nothing to worry about. When I was a little girl, I was scared too, but then I grew up and I realized there is nothing to be afraid of under the bed. There is no such thing as the boogeyman who lives under the bed. That is just a story that big kids tell to scare little kids. My big sister used to tell me that just to scare me, then she would laugh with her friends about it." Her mom walked over to the bed and messed with the pillow and blankets until they were as organized as they had been when Kayla had first climbed in.

"But mom, it's like I said, I heard it. Nobody told me something was there, I just know that it is." She pleaded with her mother to believe her.

"Look, I understand, this old bed is noisy, that's natural."

The cat had moved to the pillow and curled up on it by now looking mighty comfortable. It gave her mother an idea. "Tell you what, how about if Kitty stays in here with you tonight to protect you? Would that make you feel better?"

Kayla thought about it for a minute and it sounded better than being alone, "But Kitty will just run out when you go, mom."

"No, I'll shut the door and she'll be with you until morning. She's a tough old cat, I think you'll be safe with her. What do you say?"

"Well okay, at least I won't be all alone."

"That's right. Now I'm just gonna slip out of here and shut the door. I promise I won't tell your dad we had this conversation and we'll talk about it in the morning, okay? Now lay down."

Kayla reached behind her and picked the cat from her pillow. Then she lay back and held the cat close to her chest. Her mother pulled the blanket up to half cover the cat, then bent and kissed her on the forehead. "We'll see you girls in the morning, goodnight." And she turned and walked to the door. Kitty wriggled in Kayla's arms trying to make her exit, but she held on tight until her mom switched off the light and closed the door.

"It's just you and me now, Kitty." She said softly as she loosened her hold on the cat. "All we have to do is wait until morning."

About a half hour passed and Kayla was fast asleep. The cat lay next to her curled up on top of the blankets, purring loudly and dreaming of chasing field mice through the tall grass in the back yard. This arrangement continued until sometime after midnight.

Kayla didn't hear the scraping sounds before the cat and by the time she woke, Kitty was standing on top of her hissing, he back hunched and her fur standing on end. "What is it Kitty, what do you see?" she asked looking for her flashlight under the covers. As she frantically searched, Kitty jumped from the bed. "Noooo Kitty, don't…" she felt the cold metal of the flashlight and as she pulled it out, she flipped the switch. The beam of light shooting from the end of it made contact with the wall and illuminated the room.

Cautiously she leaned over to the side of the bed and peeked down at the floor. She could see the tail of the cat sticking out from under the bed. As she trained the beam of light on the tail, suddenly the tail disappeared under the bed as if something had grabbed it. "Rowl!" the cat howled as she heard it struggling against something unseen. Then the bed rose from the floor and landed with a thump.

She could hear hissing and growling as the cat was obviously fighting with some unseen thing and Kayla lay frozen in fear out of concern for her cat and her own safety. Another thump and the bed started to shake. Whatever was under it was obviously large and not to happy with it's current aggressor. Kayla tried to scream, but her voice wouldn't cooperate until finally another thump of the bed shook it free.

"Ahhhhhhhhh mom and dad, help! Kitty is getting killed!" she screamed louder than she thought possible. She could hear as her mom and dad scrambled up the stairs, but the sounds coming from under the bed had stopped. She was shaking and the flashlight was laying on the floor broken by the time her dad burst through the door and flipped on the light. "What the hell is going on?" he yelled as her mother came up from behind him.

"Oh my God, Troy! Look there on the floor!" she covered her mouth with her hand in disbelief.

As he father stared down at the side of the bed, Kayla finally had the nerve to look down. The flashlight lay on the floor, next to Kitty. She was sitting next to the bed, her fur ruffled and she was licking one of her paws. Beneath the other one was something she seemed intent on holding tight to the floor.

Pinned beneath her paw was a hand the size of Kayla's. It was gray and shriveled and had long black claws protruding from the tips of it's four fingers. It was opening and closing as if trying to crawl away, but Kitty was not about to let go of her trophy. As her Dad removed his shoe and pounded the thing into a bloody pulp, Kayla looked at her Mom with the look of someone who didn't have to say the words. The look said it for her. *I told you so!*

Horror Challenge Topic Suggested by:
Jenny Needham – Staple Gun
Mary Holder - A Shih Tzu

PRECIOUS MOMENTS

Janine was beside herself with fear and grief. Her beloved Shih Tzu, Precious, had run off and was missing. The dog had been playing in the back yard, where Janine had unknowingly left the gate to the fence open, and her baby got away. Now she was spending the afternoon with her staple gun and a stack of posters, putting them up on telephone poles around the community. She had decided to ride her bicycle since she had a limited area to cover, and it would be easier for her to spot her baby from the bike than from her car.

After stapling the last poster on a pole, she was making one more sweep of the neighborhood when she saw a dog that looked just like her Precious. The woman walking the dog was strolling up the sidewalk to a small house when Janine spotted her, and she had to make a wide turn to get back to the house. As she waited for a line of cars to pass, her heart was pounding in her chest. She tried to think of what she would say when the woman opened the door.

At first, she thought it would be best to be friendly, talk about her pup, and how she had wandered out of the yard. She would say, 'Thank you so much for finding her." However, by the time she got back to the house, her imagination had kicked in. As she leaned the bike against the side of the woman's porch, a terrible thought swept over her.

What if the gate had not been left open? What if the woman had stolen Precious?

The thought sent her mind reeling, and she grabbed the staple gun from the basket on her handlebars before she went to the door. She mentally prepared herself as she walked up the three steps of the porch. There was no answer when she rang the doorbell. She used the staple gun to bang on the aluminum screen door, and then hid it behind her back as she heard someone coming. The door opened just enough for the woman inside to stick her face out. "Hello. I, um, I'm looking for my dog, and..." she started.

The woman cut her off, "There ain't no dog here." She began to close the door.

Janine had to act fast. "But, she's a Shih Tzu, and I think she might be..."

"I told you, lady. I don't have a dog. Now go away." She started to close the door again.

Something inside Janine snapped and she stuck out her foot to stop the door. She didn't even know what she was about to do when she did it. With lightning speed, she whipped open the screen door and threw all of her weight against the wooden entry door. The impact sent both the woman and her tumbling into the foyer of the home. Janine recovered with a roll and came to her feet screaming, "You lying bitch! I saw you coming into this house with my Precious! Where is she?"

The woman looked terrified. "I said there's no dog here! Why don't you believe..." With a loud 'WHACK,' Janine hit her in the side of the head with the stapler and the woman fell to the floor unconscious, her head bleeding.

"Why did you have to make me do that?" Janine grabbed the woman around the waist and began dragging her toward the kitchen.

When she came to, the injured woman was sitting upright in a chair next to her dining table immobilized by the duct tape wrapped around her arms. Her ankles were taped together, and she felt uncomfortably cold from the glass of ice water that Janine had thrown at her to wake her. "Wha... what's going on?" she mumbled, trying to move her arm to her aching head.

"You know exactly what is going on. You stole my Precious, you brought her here, and you've hidden her somewhere!" Janine's eyes burned with rage as she screamed, "I've looked around, but I can't find her. Tell me where she is, and I'll take her and leave!" She pressed the staple gun against the woman's kneecap.

The woman was sobbing, "But I don't have the dog!"

"Wrong answer!" she yelled as she squeezed the trigger and shot a staple into the woman's knee.

"Aaaarrrrghh!" the woman screamed. "Please stop this! Just go! I won't call the police if you just go!"

"Damn right, you won't call the police! You gonna tell'em that you stole my dog and you're holding her captive?" She held the staple gun against the woman's forehead. "I'm the one who should call the police! You stole my dog, now tell me where she is!" She pulled the trigger again. The woman had tried to move out of the way with no success and the staple found its mark. Again she screamed as the white-hot pain of sharp steel entering her skull blurred her vision.

"Okay, okay! I'll show you where she is. Just untie me, and I'll take you to her."

"Really?" Janine's voice softened. "So, you do have her then?"

"Yes, yes, I have her. Untie me, and I'll take you to her so you can go home." The lie was barely convincing through her sobs.

Janine covered her face with her hands and rubbed her eyes. "I don't believe you! Why are you lying to me? You are just trying to get me to let you go." Moving behind the woman, she shot another staple into the back of her head.

"Awwwwhhhhh!" the woman yelled. "What do you want from me? Please! I'll do whatever you ask."

"Simple. All you have to do is tell me where she is." Janine put her mouth close to the woman's ear and whispered, "Or do I need to resort to something … more painful?"

"No, please! I can't tell you where your dog is."

"I saw you walk her right up your sidewalk. By the time I got here, you were already inside."

"But don't you see? How could I have had time to hide your dog if you saw me walking it?"

Janine was rifling through one of the kitchen drawers. "I don't know. You tell me."

"That's just it. I didn't take your dog. I didn't hide it. I don't have it!"

Janine stepped back in front of the woman brandishing a large knife she had found in the drawer. "Lady, this is your last chance." She held the knifepoint down over the woman's thigh.

The woman was so terrified that she could hardly get the words out. "I didn't…" She let out a shriek with every ounce of her lung capacity as Janine shoved the wide blade into the meat of her thigh and pulled it out releasing a gusher of blood from the wound. It appeared that the blade had severed a major artery in the woman's leg. It was obvious the pain was unbearable as she slipped out of consciousness.

"I told you it was your last chance! How stupid are you?" Janine grabbed a glass from the counter, filled it with cold water at the sink, throwing it in the woman's face. "Wake up!" she yelled.

As the woman came to, she began sobbing and trying to speak, but Janine talked over her. "That looks really bad. Give me my dog, and I'll let you get some help."

Just then the phone Janine had in the pocket of her jeans rang with a merry little ringtone. "Now what? Look lady, you have an opportunity to think about this for a minute. I need to take this call." She walked from the room, pulling the phone from her pocket. "Hello, this is Janine," she said, sounding as cheerful as she could muster.

In the kitchen, the woman struggled against the tape that bound her to the chair, but she didn't have the strength to free herself. In the other room, the caller had just enough time to give his name before the woman began calling out, "Help me! Help Me!"

"Excuse me," Janine said into the phone. "I'll be right back." She pushed the mute button on the phone and stormed back into the kitchen. "One more sound and I'll cut your damn throat, understand?" Her hand was shaking with rage as she held up the bloody knife. The woman nodded in response, whimpering and sniffling. The snot was now dripping from her nose from all her crying.

Janine held the phone back to her ear and pushed the mute button again. "Hello? Sorry about the interruption, you were saying?"

The man's voice on the other end asked, "Is everything okay there?" There was concern in his voice.

"Sorry. It's the kids. They play a little rough sometimes. So, how can I help you, Mister…"

"Canton. Jack Canton."

"Yes, Mr. Canton. How can I help you?" The forced sweetness stuck in her throat as she spoke.

"Well, ma'am, I found a poster with a picture of a dog. Had this number on it." The man's words gained impact as he spoke. "Well, I think I found your dog, and I want to bring her to you."

"What makes you think you have my dog?" She looked nervously into the kitchen.

"Well, she looks just like the picture on the poster and, when my wife called her 'Precious', she ran right to her. I'm pretty sure she's yours."

Janine didn't know what to say. She took directions to a meeting point, and said goodbye. Putting the phone back in her pocket, she walked into the kitchen. Frustrated, she slapped the woman. "Why didn't you tell me you didn't have my dog?" She kicked the woman's leg. "How stupid are you?" There was no reaction.

Janine turned on her heel and stormed out of the house. She got on her bicycle and headed down the sidewalk, leaving the motionless woman still strapped to the chair in the kitchen, her lifeless eyes turned in the direction of the open front door.

Horror Challenge Topic Suggested by:
Susan Grimm – A Vegan
Brittany Carrigan - Fried Pickles
Lisa Cagle – A Carnival

BIGGER PLANS

For twenty years, Pete had worked on the assembly line
at the car factory. He had hired on at the age of twenty-five,
two years after he had become a vegetarian. It was a lifestyle
choice that frequently invited the ridicule of his co-workers,
but he had gotten used to it. When the other members of the
crew went out for burgers, Pete would order a veggie burger
if it was available. If not, there was always the salad.
Naturally, when the guys sought to give him a nickname,
they called him Peter Rabbit.

Somewhere around the age of thirty, Pete took the next
step in his dietary progression and became a vegan. This
more restrictive diet eliminated even the kinder, gentler
animal foods like eggs and cheese and milk from his diet,
and he stopped going out with the guys completely. Instead,
he chose to bring his lunch from home. That way he always
knew what was in the food he was eating and avoided the
hassle of special ordering his lunch each day.

As he approached his twentieth anniversary at the
factory, he began talking to his friends about his dreams and
plans whenever they were on break. One day, he mentioned
that he wanted to open a fried pickle stand at the summer
carnivals. Everyone laughed.

"What's so funny about that?" he rebutted their laughter.

"Man, really? Fried pickles? There's got to be some kind of meat in that somewhere. In the grease or something," one of them suggested when the laughter died down.

"As a matter of fact, I will be using natural vegetable oils, an organic whole grain breading and organic pickles. They will be one hundred percent vegan," Pete responded with pride. "I've always loved the carnival atmosphere, and there needs to be an alternative to all the fries, funnel cakes and meat on a stick."

"Ain't no meat in fries or funnel cakes," one of them shouted over the low rumble of the factory outside the break room.

"Maybe not meat, but a lot of fries are made with beef fat to make them fry up crunchy, and funnel cakes are made with dairy products. I want to offer a vegan snack. I think it will be a popular choice in that environment."

"Fried pickles sound good to me," Nancy called out from a table in the corner.

"Yeah, well, you're pregnant, so you probably want ice cream and bacon bits on yours!" laughed Bill as he snacked on his bag of spicy pork rinds.

"Oh yeah, real funny, asshole. I think you're just jealous that Pete has a plan to get out of this place. Besides, you keep eatin' those Porkies and you won't live to be fifty." She had him with that one.

"Anyway, after next week, I'll be vested in my retirement. I've saved up the cash to get it started and I'll be out of here, travelin' with the carnival." Pete smiled and dipped another handful of pecan trail mix out of his bag.

Three weeks later, Pete walked out of the car factory for the last time. The guys had a celebration for his going away and set out a spread of lettuce and carrots as their final poke at him. He was so glad to be leaving that he played along and ended up having a good time despite the joke.

It was early May, the beginning of carnival season, when Pete got his new trailer back from the custom shop. It was beautiful, made from aluminum and stainless steel and his logo on the sides were more colorful and attractive than he expected. While he had been waiting for it to be complete, he had signed to travel with the Sutherland Brothers Carnival. It wasn't a big company, but they had a lot of what he was looking for in a troupe, including a good old-fashioned sideshow. As far as he was concerned, it was the perfect venue to get his new business off the ground.

The first day that he pulled up to the staging yard with his shiny new trailer behind his pickup truck, he got whistles and compliments from the carnies. "That there is one beautiful trailer, and it should get some attention for sure," one of the guys said as he spit tobacco juice on the ground. "You'll sure get business with that. They should put you in one of the best spots!"

"You think they will? I didn't ask about that when I signed the contract," Pete replied proudly.

"Contract? You signed the contract?" one of the women asked, looking at the others to see their expressions.

"Yeah, what's wrong with that?"

One of the guys leaned in closer and said in a low voice. "Did you read it before you signed it?"

"No, uh… they said it was the standard contract, to stay with the group for the season, split the profits, 20/80 and all that. Should I be worried?"

The same guy took him by the arm and walked him away from the group. "When you get an offer from the Devil, you usually ask questions to make sure you are getting something out of the deal before you sign. I know I did." The man looked serious.

Pete was freaked out now. He really hadn't read the paper carefully when he had signed. He had no idea what it said in the fine print. "Uhhh, really? the Devil?" He was pale and feeling sick to his stomach. That was when the man started laughing and slapped him on the back, "Don't worry, Brother. Most of us signed that paper, and we don't look like zombies, now do we?"

The whole team was in on the joke and they were all laughing. "Welcome to the show!" Pete figured he had either just been hazed by a group of strangers, or he had gotten himself into some really deep shit. He chose to go with hazing.

At the end of his first month with the show, his fried pickles proved to be wildly popular, and his profits were strong. The last night of their stint in a small town in Ohio, he was surprised when he was called to the manager's trailer. He decided it must be a good thing.

After he had broken down his trailer and packed up, he headed over to see him. Before he could knock, a booming voice called out, "Come in Pete." He opened the door and stepped in. Though it looked small on the outside, the manager's trailer seemed much larger on the inside. It was appointed with very fine and comfortable furnishings, for a carnival trailer, that is.

"Sit down, Pete. We need to talk." The heavy set, balding man motioned to the chair across from his desk. Pete saw stacks of cash from the night's receipts and felt uncomfortable being in there with all of it out in the open.

"Pete, I've heard that your pickles are a hit with the folks, and I have to tell you I am pleased with the results you are getting." The man lit a cigar. "Mind if I smoke?" he asked, and Pete shook his head no, even though he did mind.

"So you're probably wondering why I called you in tonight?" He nodded, and Pete nodded with him. "Well, my friend, it's about your contract."

"Have I done something wrong?" Pete was suddenly nervous. This was not what he had expected.

"Oh, hell no! Nothing wrong, for sure. It's just the clause on page two. I'm sure you must remember it."

"I, uh, I didn't read page two." Pete felt embarrassed to admit that he hadn't read the paper he had signed.

"Oh, that's normal. Most people don't read page two and that's a damn shame." He stared at Pete and took a long puff on his cigar. "Page two has all of the details concerning the 'success and permanence' clause."

Pete's blood chilled, "What is that?"

"Well, we like it when a new attraction is successful. In fact, we like it so much that we want your fried pickle stand to be a permanent part of the show." He had a big grin on his face, and Pete realized for the first time the big gap between the manager's two upper front teeth.

"Well, I don't know if I want to be with you for so long. I was thinking of doing the county fair circuit in the fall."

"Well, of course you were. That is why we have a contract." The manager blew a puff of smoke between his teeth and right into Pete's face, causing him to cough. "You really should have read it before you signed on the line, Peter Rabbit."

Pete felt a twinge of panic now. "How did you know that people called me that at the plant?"

"I know everything about you, Mr. Rabbit. I know how you became a vegan, how you stole money from your mother when she was passed out drunk, how you looked in your neighbor Patty's windows and watched her getting undressed when you were thirteen. Need I go on?"

Pete shook his head. "No, but I don't feel so well. I need to go now."

"Of course you do, Mr. Rabbit. That's what they all say." The manager's face became distorted and his eyes glowed red with intensity. He began mocking Pete. "I don't feel well. Waah, waah, waah." He chuckled. "You don't know how many times I've heard that. The guy with the funnel cake cart, the woman who owned the Tilt-a-Whirl, even the french fry guy said the same pathetic words, right before they left. Well, some of them left, except for a couple of folks in the sideshow."

Pete opened his mouth to answer but could only make a pathetic bleating sound. It seemed as though the man and his desk were growing larger in front of him. He felt dizzy as he noticed that the chair he was sitting in was expanding as well. His head dropped forward and he got a look at his feet. *Was that fur?* He wanted to run, but he was aching so badly he just sat there his sides heaving as he tried to slow his breathing and calm down.

"There, there, Mr. Rabbit," the man said as he scooped Pete up in his large hand. "It's not so bad. The french fry guy gave me a lot of grief, and he still isn't happy in the sideshow, but we needed a two headed turtle. Too bad our magician already has a rabbit." As he was apologizing, he opened the door of the trailer and tossed Pete out onto the damp grass. "Thanks for the pickle idea. I never would have thought that something like that would be so wildly popular." Then he slammed the door shut.

When the sun rose the next morning, the caravan pulled out of the park where they had been set up for the last four days. With it was the shiny trailer with the colorful pickle logo on the sides. All that remained was an assortment of scattered trash blowing in the wind, sawdust that had been scattered on the ground around the amusements, and a rabbit named Pete. A gentle soul who had given up everything for a dream and now would spend the rest of his days living the vegan lifestyle he had chosen many years before.

Horror Challenge Topic Suggested by:
Jennifer Warrick Davis: An old oil painting

DARK MASTERPIECE

Bruce was a dumpster diver. If you were to call him that to his face, he wouldn't be angry. He would simply recite the laundry list of treasures he had discovered while enjoying his favorite activity. There was the barely used vacuum cleaner, the set of twenty-five office chairs, the lamps, old records, and, oh yeah, the Rolex watch. Well, it wasn't a real Rolex, but it looked real enough from a distance. He had worn that watch proudly for years until the band had finally broken. When that happened, he sent it back to the smelly resting place where he had come into possession of it.

Today was going well for him. He had uncovered a whole box of DVD cases, a really nice jacket with matching pants in a dry cleaning bag, and a few oak boards. He was daydreaming about the boards when he found his biggest prize ever – a very old looking painting in a beautiful gilded frame. When he spotted it, he got so excited he jumped out of his small pickup truck without first shifting it into park. As he stood there admiring his new find, his truck began to roll away.

"Damn!" he said, holding on to the painting and running for the truck. When he caught up to it, the door was still open so he jumped in and pushed the brake pedal down hard. The truck stopped immediately only inches from a brick wall. His heart was pounding as he pressed his back against the seat and pulled himself together. He was still clutching the painting, so he carefully set it on the floor, leaning it against the seat to keep it from falling over. After a moment he put the truck in reverse, turned around and headed for home.

All the way home Bruce thought about the painting. He couldn't help but steal a glance at it from time to time whenever he could take his eyes off the road. He wondered if it was a valuable painting. It looked very old, but it could be an imitation painted by someone local. Then he would have a flash of rational thought, and his mind would convince him that it was probably of no value at all. Why would it be sitting behind a plaza next to a dumpster if it was worth anything?

When he got home, he left everything else in the truck and carried his treasure into the house. He walked straight to the living room wall, took down an existing picture of a boat sailing on the ocean and hung the old painting on the wall. Finally he could get a good look at it.

It was a slightly faded portrait of an incredibly beautiful young woman. Her clothing was from a much earlier time and, if Bruce had to guess, he would have said it was Victorian. She wore a large hat topped with long colorful feathers. Surrounding her was something like dark smoke. It swirled somewhat transparently over the common highlights of a woman's physique as if to gently caress her, and the sly smile on her face suggested she might be enjoying herself as she posed for the artist. Bruce felt a twinge in his stomach as he stared at her and she seemed to stare back.

In that one breathless moment he felt as though he must be the luckiest man in the entire world, it was a euphoric feeling he had never before experienced. He felt warm, full and satisfied. He felt joy and sensed that he was loved. Loved? Holy crap! This beautiful woman loved him. Ahead and above any other man she could have, she loved him!

How could he turn and walk away from something so perfect, so incredible?

He could not.

The sun set in the world outside his small home, but he did not notice. It rose again the next morning, and he took no note of the rays as they fell through the window and passed across the room until they fell upon the painting. He felt a near panic in the depths of his spirit as he moved quickly to stand between the sun and the woman.

It was the first time he had moved at all since he had hung the painting on the wall. He had a sense that he must protect her at all costs, but he did not understand why. However, with that simple act of chivalry, he was rewarded with another wave of joy and love washed over him. When the sunlight melted away and the shadows extended across the room a few hours later, still Bruce continued to stand and stare.

In the middle of the night, as he stood there enraptured, suddenly she spoke to him. "I wish to express my gratitude for your act of kindness and concern." *Had her head turned as she spoke to him?* "You are deserving much more than any other has ever offered. I give you my love, Bruce, my body and my soul." At once she fell silent.

He was so happy. She had expressed her love assuring him that she felt as he did. Body and soul, he was hers as well. It was like no other love he had ever known or known about. Such a perfect bond, the feeling of being one with the woman made only for him, stroke by brush stroke.

When the sun rose on the third day, there was a knock on the door. At first he did not hear it, and then he ignored it, but the knocking persisted. Just as he shifted his weight to go to the door, the woman in the portrait appealed to him,

"Why would you leave me now? I have given myself to you and yet you would turn your back on me?"

Bruce had not spoken for days but he managed to push a word up from his diaphragm and through his parched vocal cords, "Never."

Finally, the person at the door went away and left him alone with his love. He was grateful for the silence, the removal of even the slightest distraction. Throughout the day and following night, he continued to stand there basking in the waves of passion that washed over him causing him at times to quake with sheer joy. His mind swirled in revelry and his eyes locked in her gaze. Days and nights passed and his eyes refused to close. He stood frozen before the portrait. The pool of urine at his feet had long since dried and the weight of his clothes hung on him though his mind refused to acknowledge it.

One day there came a knock at the door again. This time Bruce could not hear it for the ringing, rather the singing in his ears. He was unaware that just outside the door was his only friend, a guy he had once worked with couple of jobs ago. It was a friend who refused to give up and go away. Instead the visitor walked around to the back door and took a look into the back of Bruce's truck. What he saw was alarming – items of value, and out in the open. Bruce would never leave anything worth anything in the back of his truck.

He went up to the door, but instead of knocking, he tried the doorknob, which happened to be open. He walked in and called out, "Bruce? Dude? It's me." His stomach churned as the stench of urine and feces overpowered him. He expected to find that his friend was dead but, when he walked into the living room, there was Bruce staring at a painting on the wall. Although it wasn't exactly Bruce standing there, it was someone resembling Bruce and dressed in Bruce's clothes.

The sunken facial features of his mesmerized friend had taken on a decidedly feminine appearance, but that was not what was most startling. The painting on the wall was a portrait of a man in Victorian clothing and a large hat adorned with a long feather. His face looked remarkably like Bruce. Unsure of what to do, he stood in front of the portrait and grabbed the person standing there. He yelled, "Bruce, or whoever you are, what is going on here?"

Slowly, the person turned to face him and, with parched, cracked lips, she smiled. The strange person definitely was not Bruce and surely was a woman. "What happened here?" he asked her. Her hand moved to her throat and she said, "Drink."

Bruce's friend ran to get her a glass of water. Holding the glass with both hands, the woman nearly emptied it before lowering it from her lips. Now he asked her again, "What is going on here? Where is Bruce?"

She looked at him for a long time before answering. "I am his sister, Julia. Bruce has been called away... a family emergency. He has instructed me that if anyone came by, I should tell them that he does not know when he'll return."

"Okay, but that doesn't explain your condition, and why you didn't answer the door."

"I apologize. I am subject to seizures from time to time and it can linger for days. But I am fine now. I just need some time alone to recover. I am sure you understand." She looked deep into his eyes.

"Oh, yeah, sure. I'll be on my way now and come by tomorrow to make sure you're okay."

"Yes, that will be good." She motioned toward the door. "So I will see you tomorrow then?"

"Okay, I'll see you tomorrow." He headed for the door.

As soon as she was certain he had gone, she searched the house for a bathtub, and cleaned herself up. She was happy to put on some clean clothes and find the kitchen so she could make herself something to eat. Recovered now, she searched the house for money and anything else of value. She put what she found in a bag, grabbed the painting from the wall, and exited the house through the back door. Walking down the street carrying the portrait and the bag, she ducked down an alley behind a plaza and she deposited the painting next to a dumpster.

"Thank you, Bruce, for releasing me from this prison. I am sorry that I have to leave you now, but if you are lucky maybe someone will find you and take you home and love you like you did me." She smiled then, "I only had to wait a half century for you to find me and love me. Maybe you won't have to wait so long. It's all in the love, you know. That is the key that will release you." She laughed, brushed the hair from her eyes, and walked back out to the street where she disappeared into her new world.

Horror Challenge Topic Suggested by:
Duncan McGonall - an old, worn pair of work boots

SIXTEEN TONS

Glenn was at his mother's house helping her clean out the basement when they came upon a medium-sized wooden trunk that looked to be more than a hundred years old. "Wow, that is some piece of work!" he marveled as he looked the trunk over. "Where did this come from?"

"You know what, Honey? I put that trunk away a long time ago after your grandfather died in the coal mine accident." She glanced over at her son realizing how he had grown into quite a handsome man. "You look a lot like him, you know," she said wistfully. "Anyway, I was saving his things for you so one day you might get to know him a bit. You were so young when he died."

"I don't remember him at all." Glenn felt a pang of regret that he could not share the memories of his grandfather with her. "I was, what? Two years old when he died?"

"Somewhere around there, but you and he hit it off from the moment he first laid eyes on you in the hospital. He loved to play with you when we went for a visit. Your cousins used to get so jealous!" She reached over and touched his chin as she spoke. "Then came the collapse at the mine, and we lost him." Quiet for a moment, she regained her composure. "But I saved this trunk, and all of the things in it, so one day you could get to know him again."

"So, do you have the key to the lock?" He was dying to see what could be inside.

"Oh no, it isn't locked. Your grandfather just put the lock on it for decoration, not to keep people out. It's open."

Glenn carried the sturdy trunk out to the open area in the middle of the room and lifted the lid. It was a veritable treasure chest of relics from his grandfather's life. There was a stack of black and white photos tied together with string, several coins and small souvenirs from parts of the world that he had traveled during the war. Buried farther down were some cufflinks and other small items a man might take from his pockets at the end of a long day. There was one mystery item – a paper bag with something heavy in it.

Going straight for the bag, Glenn opened it carefully letting the smell of old leather waft out. "Boots?" He sat back, a little disappointed with the find.

"Those were his last pair of work boots." His mother pulled them out of the bag. "He was wearing these when the accident happened. He literally died in these boots."

She noticed the look of confusion on his face. "I bet I know what you are thinking. Why keep the boots he died in, right?"

"Damn, mom! You know me so well! That's exactly, well... almost exactly what I was thinking."

"Whenever anyone was critical about somebody else, your grandfather had a habit of replying, 'You can never understand a man and what he's made of until you've worn his boots.' He said it so often that I thought it was the perfect way for you to know him." She blushed. "I know. It's a little weird, isn't it? But he would've liked it."

"No, Mom. It makes a lot of sense." He took the boots from her and put them back in the bag. "Can I take this stuff home with me later and go through it?"

"That was the point of keeping it, dear. Of course you can."

Glenn put the bag back in the trunk and set it near the stairway to carry it up later. He and his mother took the rest of the afternoon to finish the cleanup.

Later that night, at his apartment, he carried the trunk to his coffee table to go through it. He took everything out and laid it out on the table, setting the bag with the boots on the floor. Untying the stack of photos, he took time to look at each one. Some had names and dates on the back while others did not. He had seen photos of his grandfather before, so he recognized him right off, but there were men with him in some of the photos that were not identified. Glenn assumed they were friends of the family.

After picking up each item and looking it over, he carefully placed it back into the trunk. The only thing left now was the boots in the bag. After moving the trunk from the table to the floor, he took the boots from the bag and set them on the table. The boots were in pretty good shape considering what they must have been through, and they seemed to have been cleaned and polished before they were stored. No need to be concerned about getting coal dust on his furniture or carpet. He stared at them for a long minute, then said, "Oh hell, why not?"

One at a time, Glenn put his feet up on the table and removed his sports shoes. He put on one boot, then the other, and pulled the laces tight. He tied them like every other shoe he had ever worn. He stood and walked across the room and then sat down again. They fit perfectly and were surprisingly comfortable. He put his feet up on the table and looked at them again. *Man, these are pretty cool. I could probably wear these with jeans.* He nodded to himself at the thought.

He was feeling tired after the cleaning they had done earlier, and he leaned back and closed his eyes. Suddenly, the darkness felt oppressive. It was hard to breathe and the air was cool and stale. There was an eerie silence except for the sound of breathing... his and someone else's.

"Who's there?" he called into the darkness. It startled Glenn to hear a different voice coming out of his throat.

"It's Jack... Art, you doin' alright?"

"Oh yeah. Sorry, I forgot where I was for a second. How's Manny doin'?"

"You sure you're okay?" Jack sounded genuinely concerned. "The slide, it crushed him. Manny's gone, Art, remember? I tried to dig him out, but when I saw how his chest was crushed, I gave it up."

"Sorry, man. My mind's in and out. How long've we been down here, do you think?"

"Not sure, maybe ten days." Jack started coughing, "I can't tell if anyone is even trying to get to us. Can you hear anything?"

"Nothin'. I'm friggin' starving."

"Me too. We're gonna starve to death down here if we don't eat. There's still air and water for now, but I don't have any fat to live on anymore."

"I know, Jack. You was always pretty thin anyway."

"Look, I was thinkin', if we had something to eat, we might be able to last long enough till they can get to us." His voice softened to a whisper. "Look, Art, this is gonna sound crazy, but..."

"I know what you're gonna say. I remember thinkin' about it, maybe a day or two ago I think."

"Manny?" Jack didn't say more.

"Yeah. I don't know. I feel like if it was me over there, he might feel the same way about it. Like I think he'd be okay with it."

"He'd probably tell ya to eat his privates!" Jack started laughing, ending up with a coughing fit.

"Yeah. That'd be Manny all right."

The darkness fell silent between them.

Finally, Glenn lifted his head. "So what do you think?"

"I think we should light up to decide."

Glenn could hear as a lighter was opened and saw the flashes as it was lit. The light hurt his eyes as they adjusted to the sudden brightness, and the face of the other man came into focus. He was holding the lighter up to something and the light spread throughout the small cavern where they sat. Jack handed the lighter over and, as Glenn reached out, he observed it was his grandfather's hands that took the lighter and lit the lamp on his hardhat.

"I don't know. You sure we need to do this?" His grandfather's voice sounded raspy and more than a little shaky.

"I don't think we have much choice, Art," replied the other man. "First, we gotta find him."

The two men stood, crouching below the low ceiling of the mine. Glenn followed the other man, stepping carefully across the rocks and debris, about twenty feet toward the body of their friend.

"Manny…" Jack said in a faltering voice as he crawled in closer to the dead man. "We need you to help us out here. Me and Art is gonna starve if we don't do what we gotta do."

"We're sorry, Manny, but I swear, we'll take care of your family if we get outta this mess." Art was trying to control his emotions as he spoke.

"Yeah," Jack agreed. "We'll do everything we can to make sure they have what they need."

Jack pulled a knife from his pocket and moved even closer to the man whose partially buried body jutted out from under the coal and large wooden beam that flattened his chest. The smell of human decomposition caused Glenn to feel sick to his stomach, but Jack went to work cutting the man's pant leg exposing a section of his leg from ankle to knee. When Jack cut into the purple flesh, thick black blood oozed from the wound. "I'm sorry, buddy." He sobbed as he sawed off a chunk of the meat and passed it toward Glenn before cutting some off for himself.

Glenn sat on the hard rock floor and stared at the raw piece of his friends leg in his hand for what seemed like an hour. Finally, he took a bite of the tough meat. He had to pull hard to work the bite loose from the larger chunk. It tasted bad and, as he began to chew, he was overcome by dry heaves and spit it back out into his hand. There was nothing in his stomach for him to throw up. "God forgive us!" He said and forced himself to eat what he had bitten off.

Glenn awoke on the sofa with his feet still resting on the table wearing the boots. He was sick to his stomach and ran to the bathroom where his full stomach had no problem bringing something up. He wiped the sweat from his brow and cleaned himself up. After removing the boots and placing them back in the bag, he reached for the phone and dialed his mother. Opening the trunk as he waited, he pulled out the old photos again.

"Hello." His mother answered the phone.

"Mom, I need to ask you about grandfather…" He stopped to consider how he should word the question.

"Yes, dear, what is it?"

"Uhhh, when they found him in the mine, who else was with him? Do you know?" As he finished the question, he found the photo he had passed over before.

"Yes, Glenn. It was his friend, Jack. He used to come to the house for family picnics. We called him Uncle Jack. Why do you ask? Do you remember him?"

"Was it only the two of them who were trapped?" He turned the photo over to read the writing on the back.

"Yes, Honey. There was another man as well, but they never found his body. I don't remember his name."

"Manny?" He read the names on the back of the photo: *Manny, Jack, and Dad.*

"Yes, I think that was his name. The three of them were always together. What's wrong Glenn?"

"Well... Nothing, Mom, but it's true what Grandpa said about wearing another man's boots. You never really know a man until you wear them. I love you, Mom. I'll talk to you later."

"I love you too, Honey. Good night. Oh, and Glenn?"

"Yeah, Mom?"

"I know this kind of thing can cause some strong feelings, but try not to let it eat at you, okay?"

Glenn coughed. "Yeah, thanks Mom. Bye."

If you enjoyed these stories, you may want to try the full-length novels, and novellas written by JH Glaze. Available on Amazon.com - in eBook and Paperback, & other online retailers in Paperback format.

Adult Horror:
The Paranormal Adventures of John Hazard Novels
The Spirit Box: John Hazard Book I
NorthWest: John Hazard Book II
Send No Angel: John Hazard Book III
Ghost Wars: John Hazard Book IV (*Coming 2014*)

Special Novellas: YA & Adult
Forced Intelligence: A Novella.
The Life We Dream: A Novella.

Serial Novel: YA & Adult
RUNE: The Thriller Series:

Visit the websites and pages of JH Glaze:
www.JHGlaze.com
https://www.facebook.com/JHGlaze.author
Twitter: @themostcoolone
Search for JH Glaze on Google for more!

Thanks For Reading!